OWN THE EIGHTS

OWN THE EIGHTS: BOOK ONE

KRISTA SANDOR

CANDY CASTLE BOOKS

PROLOGUE

"Are you waiting for someone?"

Georgiana Jensen glanced up at the bartender. "Yes, I am," she answered, then looked toward the entrance of the cozy bistro, only to find a young couple waving to a group of people at a table near the front of the restaurant.

In the up-and-coming Tennyson neighborhood, not far from the bookstore she'd recently opened thanks to a small business loan and emptying her savings, the bistro felt like the perfect little rendezvous spot, buzzing with conversation and the possibility of new things.

Georgie could just feel it. Her life was about to change.

"I'm Irene," the bartender said, brushing her bangs from her eyes.

"Georgiana, well, Georgie is what most everyone calls me."

The woman nodded. "I feel like I've seen you around."

"I just moved to the area. I own the little bookstore a few blocks down."

Irene slapped the bar. "That's it! Jensen's Books, right?"

A warmth filled her chest. "Yep, that's my shop."

The bartender gestured to the cocktail napkin on the

counter's polished surface. "Are you doing okay tonight, Georgie?"

Once a perfect, crisp square, Georgie had decimated the poor thing, working out her nervous energy, tearing and twisting the white paper into a little pile of sad confetti.

She felt her cheeks heat. "I'm sorry. I'm a little nervous."

"Blind date?" the bartender asked, brushing the white fragments into her hand.

Georgie shook her head. "No, we met at a housewarming party last night."

Irene smiled. "That's got to be a good sign to meet at a party and then make plans to see each other the next day."

Georgie couldn't hold back her grin. It wasn't just a good sign. It was perfect.

Her mind drifted to last night. She'd arrived late to the party. It was honestly a miracle she'd gone at all. She wasn't the party type, never had been. At twenty-five years old, she had more in common with the Golden Girls, minus Blanche, than a party girl. But when she'd bumped into an old college acquaintance earlier in the day, and the woman had insisted she come to the gathering, Georgie found herself saying yes instead of her typical no.

And that's where she'd met Brice Casey.

Perfection wrapped into one man.

They'd talked all night.

Scratch that.

She hadn't talked much.

Extremely loquacious and undeniably handsome, Brice filled the space between them with his sparkling smile and shining green eyes. He spoke of his job—he was already a VP at his father's company at the age of twenty-nine—and he drank Manhattans, which seemed sophisticated compared to the bottle of eight-dollar Chardonnay she'd picked up on her way to the gathering.

It wasn't her fault she didn't know the first thing about wine and spirits. Her Friday nights were spent baking muffins with her nose buried deep in a book as the warm, comforting scents of chocolate and cinnamon filled her modest bungalow. The fictional characters Lizzie Bennet, Jane Eyre, and Hermione Granger kept her company while the rest of the twenty-some-things scoured the clubs in search of finding *the one*.

But something had made her take a chance and agree to attend this party.

She and Brice had spoken, well, *he'd* spoken, for nearly two hours before the low hum of an incoming text stopped him mid-sentence, and he told her he had to leave. It did seem strange that he'd have a family emergency at quarter to one in the morning, but when he'd asked for her number and suggested they meet for drinks tonight, all her worries melted away.

In the age of dating apps and low expectations, it seemed almost primitive that she'd met someone at an actual gathering of quasi-adults. There were a group of gentlemen doing keg stands in the small backyard, but Brice didn't seem like those overgrown man-boys. No, Brice was going places. He'd actually told her that, several times. He'd also mentioned he was quite a catch, which he certainly seemed to be.

Georgie released a slow breath. He must have seen something in her. This perfect man must have seen the woman behind the glasses and the messy bun. And while she hadn't shared much about herself—she'd used the only opening in the conversation which occurred when Brice stopped talking to pop a mini quiche into his mouth, to excuse herself to use the restroom after having to pee for nearly an hour. But Brice was waiting for her with a fresh drink in his hand when she emerged, empty-bladdered.

Come to think of it, he'd had quite a few fresh drinks while they were chatting.

No matter.

Tonight, she was drinking club soda. There wasn't going to be any eight-dollar Chardonnay clouding her mind. No, if this was going to be the biggest night of her life, she wanted to remember every detail with crystal clear clarity.

"That might be him," the bartender said with a slight nod toward the door.

Georgie's pulse ratcheted up a notch. "Is it a guy?"

"Yeah, and he's scanning the place."

"Does he have perfect hair and a broad chest?"

Irene nodded. "I'll give you that. The hair is pretty great."

Georgie swallowed past the lump in her throat.

You can do this. You've had hundreds, even thousands of pairs of eyes watching you. Brice Casey is one guy. You've got this.

She turned on the barstool and plastered on her best beauty queen smile. She'd use every little tool in her arsenal tonight—even the ones she'd promised herself she'd never resurrect.

Brice's gaze passed over her once, then twice, then a third time before it landed on a group of giggling women in a booth, knocking back tequila shooters.

"Brice! Over here!" she called and raised her hand like she was the biggest nerd in class.

Well, she was the biggest nerd, but no bother. He'd picked her, right? This handsome man, with what he'd described as a bevy of prospects, liked her.

He took a few steps forward and narrowed his gaze. "Virginia?"

She looked from side to side and caught Irene's eye. The woman grimaced then moved down the bar to serve a hipster holding up an empty beer stein.

"Georgiana," she said, patting her chest as if she were introducing herself to a long-hidden away Amazonian tribe who'd never come into contact with others.

"Georgia?" Brice said on another try.

Holy Mary!

"Close," she answered, turning up the wattage on her smile. "Georgie is what most people call me. Only my mother calls me Georgiana, but we don't have to get into her on our first date," she added with a high-pitched laugh that sounded like a horse whinnying on helium.

Get it together, girl!

Brice looked her up and down. "I must have had on some serious beer goggles last night. You are not what I remember."

Hermione, Lizzie, and Jane, her fictional soul sisters, shook their imaginary heads and Georgie's jaw dropped.

She steadied herself and had a quick tête-à-tête with the fictional trifecta.

He didn't just say that I'd been more attractive after a few drinks, did he?

The literary trio answered by clucking their tongues.

She had to have misheard him.

She tried to amp her grin up, but she'd hit deranged beauty queen, and there was no going past that.

"You were drinking Manhattans, not beer. Remember, you told me the story about how you and your fraternity brothers drove all the way from Denver to New York to have an authentic experience ordering the drink in the real Manhattan?"

Brice nodded, and his expression grew nostalgic. "Those, Virginia, those were good days."

"It's Georgiana. Georgie," she corrected, her smile deflating like a balloon.

This was not the perfect date she'd envisioned.

"I would have sworn it was Virginia," he answered, scratching his chin.

"No, my name's Georgie. It always has been."

"You're sure it's not Georgia?"

She stared into his beautiful eyes. Should she just let him call her Georgia? It was close to Georgie.

Hermione groaned somewhere in her subconscious.

Georgie mustered every ounce of self-worth she had. "Yes, I'm completely positive that my name is Georgiana. Well, Georgie."

"Really, huh? Georgie? It does sound a lot like Georgia," he added with a slight smirk as if he'd just cured world hunger on the fly.

She needed to change tack. "Did you want to get something to eat or maybe a drink first?"

Brice's gaze slid toward the table of laughing women and then back to her. "I'm going to level with you, Georgia."

"Georgie," she corrected, feeling the walls closing in on her.

He patted her shoulder with the tenderness of a salamander. "Listen, Georgia, I'm going to go. This isn't going to work for me."

Georgie glanced at his hand and then to his stunning face. "I'm not sure I understand."

He shook his head and sighed dramatically, feigning compassion. "It's me. It's not you."

Her heart stopped beating. Okay, it didn't stop. She was still standing, but it surely hiccupped at Brice's words.

"Oh, I see. I just thought because you asked to meet me tonight that we..." she trailed off, but it didn't matter because Brice wasn't even listening to her. His gaze was locked on the tequila shooter contingent...again.

"Brice?" she said.

His head snapped back, and he waved his hands. "No, I got that wrong."

Georgie held her breath. "You did?"

"Yeah, I did...because it is you. You see, I'm going places, Virginia, and people expect a certain caliber of woman on my arm."

Caliber of woman?

Georgie's literary trifecta bristled.

"Excuse me?" she bit out, the words barely a whisper.

He took a step back and looked her up and down. "The truth is, Georgia, you're an eight at best."

A flurry of judges' scorecards and the dull ache of wearing five-inch heels for twelve hours straight washed over her.

"An eight?" she echoed.

"Yeah, like on a scale from—"

She put up her hand. "Oh, I understand what you're telling me."

Brice's perfect features came together in a condescending grin. "Good, I'm glad. And you should own it, Virginia."

"The eight?" she shot back.

"Sure, I mean, it won't get you a guy like me, but there's gotta be someone out there good with an eight."

The room started to spin. The lights were suddenly too bright, highlighting her every fault, her tiniest of blemishes. She could smell the Aqua Net, feel the Vaseline smeared across her teeth.

You need to get the fuck out of there.

Georgie blinked. Prim and proper Jane Eyre just dropped an f-bomb.

"So, we're good? No hard feelings, Georgia?"

Brice Casey had a beautiful face with a strong jawline and a sweet little dimple that winked every time he cracked a smile. He smelled good, and he dressed like a GQ cover model.

And she couldn't be more disappointed with herself if she'd tried.

She, more than anyone, should know better than to judge

someone on their appearance. She knew the trappings of perfection all too well.

But here's what really stung. Brice Casey may be a first-class asshat, but she was the one who fell for his good looks, hook, line, and sinker.

Deep in her mind, Lizzie, Jane, and Hermione were shaking their fictional heads.

Georgie lifted her chin. "Yeah, we're good, Brice."

"Ah, you're a peach. Hey, like a Georgia peach," he said, his eyes lighting up at his cleverness before he turned and left the bistro.

She watched the door slam then looked over her shoulder to see Irene.

"No dice on the date?" the woman asked with a sympathetic expression.

"He said I was just an eight and not the *caliber* of girl he usually dated."

Irene sucked in a tight breath. "Ouch! Are you okay?"

Georgie straightened her shoulders. "You know what? I'm fine. It just took the perfect jerk to help me see it."

"Girl power," the bartender said, extending her closed hand for a fist bump.

Georgie reciprocated. "Girl power."

"And you should own that eight, lady," Irene said with a chuckle, slapping a dish towel over her shoulder.

Georgie stilled. "That's what he said."

"What? That guy?" Irene asked.

"Yeah, he said I should own it."

The bartender shrugged. "Own the Eights? It is kind of catchy."

An idea sparked in Georgie's mind, and her three fictional mavens shrieked with excitement.

"It is," Georgie answered, her thoughts racing. She glanced

down at the half-empty glass, determination coursing through her veins. "What do I owe you for the club soda?"

Irene waved her off. "On the house. An eights special."

Georgie grabbed her purse off the back of the stool, passed the tequila gigglers, and left the bistro. The gentle hum of the restaurant trailed behind her until all she heard were the quick snippets of conversation as she weaved her way home through couples and groups out for a night on Tennyson Street.

Block by block, she made her way down the main drag, then headed up a tree-covered side street toward a row of sleepy bungalows. With each step, a plan, no a religion, well, not a religion in the whole holiness scheme of things, but a way of thinking percolated in her mind. A philosophy to live by that would help women ignore blinding attractiveness and weed through the GQ jerks so they could focus on what really mattered.

Substance.

Character.

Kindness.

Intelligence.

And she was not about to keep this relationship epiphany to herself.

"Oh, I'll show you how to own the eights," she said, all determination and gumption, unlocking her front door as the clickity-clack of paws prancing on hardwood thundered toward her.

Black and white with one ear cocked up while the other drooped down, Mr. Tuesday, her sweet mutt-du jour, met her at the door with a wet nose and a warm kiss. She scratched behind his ears, then eyed her laptop on the living room table.

She picked up the device and settled in on the couch with Mr. Tuesday curled up next to her.

"Maybe we should make some coffee. I have a feeling this is going to be a late night."

Mr. Tuesday let out a doggie sigh and closed his eyes. He wasn't going to be any help. He still ate her shoes and never met a squirrel he wouldn't chase. But she loved her shelter pup all the same.

She glanced around the room. "I need to get something."

She set the laptop aside, went to her closet, and pulled out a worn shoebox. Opening the lid, she removed a wallet-sized snapshot and went back to the couch.

"This will be my reminder, Mr. Tuesday," she said, giving the picture one more look before sliding it into the back of her wallet.

Opening her laptop, she pulled up the page for CityBeat, the internet's mecca for lifestyle blogging. "All right, let's do this. Enter name of blog," she read aloud.

Her fingertips tingled.

"Oh, I've got a name for a blog. A name and a revolutionary way of thinking that will help the women of the world navigate the treacherous trail of handsome douchebags and find real, lasting love," she said to the sweet pup, now snoring peacefully.

She steepled her hands, cracked her knuckles, then typed three words.

Own the Eights.

Tagline: *Why date a ten when you should marry the eight.*

She stared at the screen. "That'll get people's attention."

And with the power and determination of a woman done with the guise of perfection who was not named Virginia or Georgia, Georgiana Jensen hit enter.

1

GEORGIE

"Today's the day you find out if you won or not, right, Georgie?"

Georgiana set a stack of books on the counter, twisted her dark tangle of hair into a lopsided bun, then began sorting through a stack of unpaid bills.

Busy. She had to stay busy, or her nerves would get the best of her.

Georgie tapped the stack of bills into a neat pile. They'd get paid...eventually. And hopefully, if things went her way, she'd be caught up in no time. She set the stack back on the shelf beneath the bookshop's register and turned to her part-time employee and her friend Irene's little sister, Becca Murphy.

"Yeah, the last email I received said I should find out today if they chose me."

Georgie glanced at her phone, which had remained silent for the better part of the day. She'd already checked her email eight thousand times. What would one more look hurt? She tapped the envelope icon and found...nothing.

No new emails.

Becca bent over and patted Mr. Tuesday's head. "What do you think, Mr. Tuesday? Is Georgie going to be the next super-blogger for CityBeat? Is her blog going to be broadcast to all gazillion of the CityBeat readers?"

Mr. Tuesday's ears perked up, and he barked.

"See, even your dog agrees that you've got this," Becca said with a wide grin.

Georgie played with the tie on her apron. For the sake of the shop and her livelihood, Mr. Tuesday better be right. At this point, winning the CityBeat contest was her best prospect for keeping the bookstore open.

Nearly two years ago to the day, Georgie had started the Own the Eights blog on CityBeat's site. The night of her encounter with Brice Casey had ignited a firestorm within her. She'd typed and typed, recounting the humiliating event and filled her first post with dating advice and the pitfalls of perfection.

Because that's what perfection was. A false construct. A facade.

She'd thought Brice had been the perfect catch. But she'd been blinded by his good looks. Thanks to the guidance of her fictional trifecta, she'd decided to write a blog that would help others *not* make the same mistake she had and teach them how to weed out the superficial aspects of dating to ensure a deeper level of connection.

Beauty is only skin deep, and it didn't last forever. Forget initial attraction. Screw chemistry.

To hell with society's version of perfection! Kindness, respect, and integrity were the real building blocks of a relationship. Her plan boiled down to this, write out the ten qualities you'd want in your ideal mate, then cross off the two that had anything to do with physical perfection.

Now, you had your eight substantive qualities to seek out in a significant other. A beacon of information that pointed you away from the empty flash of a perfect ass or the initial titillation of a charming grin and into the arms of the person who'd see in you what really mattered—your heart and your soul.

Georgie hadn't even proofread the manifesto before hitting publish. Exhausted from penning her unabomber-esque declaration, she and her trusty companion, Mr. Tuesday, had crashed right there on the sofa. It was only when Mr. Tuesday dropped his slobber-encrusted ball on her sleeping face at the ass crack of dawn that she peeled her eyes open and found herself knee-deep in the world of relationship and lifestyle blogging.

Within twenty-four hours of the Own the Eights blog going live, she had thousands of followers and the Own the Eights hashtag had begun trending on social media. People everywhere posted their top ten list with the most superficial qualities crossed off.

Spurred by her success, Georgie's blog grew to include an advice post every Wednesday, articles on where to meet your true soul mate and even included recipes, volunteer opportunities, inspirational meditations, and a list of suggested books to read. Between running her bookshop and writing the blog, she'd barely had a moment to breathe.

Unfortunately, while she loved blogging, it didn't pay the bills...until, possibly, now.

"So, what happens next?" Becca asked.

Georgie closed her eyes and took a steadying breath. "The last email from CityBeat said to offer up some activities and then write about how they're in-line with the tone of our blog. I sent them a few ideas for where to meet a quality partner and ways to stay centered while you're waiting to find your eight."

"And that's it? If you win, they'll start paying you?"

Georgie nodded. "The winner gets ten thousand dollars up-front and then gets brought on as a paid contributor."

"Wow, Georgie!" Becca exclaimed. "That's huge!"

But there was more. A *more* Georgie thought about right

before she fell asleep every night since she'd entered the contest. Most of CityBeat's paid contributors went on to write books, host talk shows, headline as speakers at events. They made a difference on a grand scale, reaching people all over the world. If she won, not only could she afford to keep the shop open, she could help people find true love just like her literary trifecta—not just in the pages of a book, but in real life.

Becca leaned against the counter. "Earth to Georgie. When are you supposed to do all these activities?"

Georgie snapped back from her make-it-big daydream and glanced at the calendar on the wall. "Over the next few weeks. And I meant to ask you. Do you mind working more hours if I get picked for this? The email said there may be additional blog posts I'll need to write and events I'll need to attend. It sounds like I'll need to be at their beck and call during this time."

Becca's eyes lit up. "Are you kidding? I'm a poor college student on summer break. Hell yes, I'll take the hours," she answered as the door to the bookshop opened, and a line of gray-haired women entered while a man with a cane held the door for them.

The new arrivals smiled warmly and made themselves comfortable in the seating area at the front of the shop.

"How are you doing, Georgie? Have you found out if you got it?" one of the women asked, breaking away from the group and coming to the counter.

"They haven't announced anything yet, Mrs. Gilbert," she answered, trying to stay calm.

The woman nodded, then addressed the group who were settling themselves into the worn chairs. "Everyone, listen!" Mrs. Gilbert called out at the top of her lungs, causing Georgie and Becca to nearly fall over. "They haven't announced the winner yet!" She turned back to them with an apologetic grin. "My husband's hearing aid is on the fritz again, so I've had to raise my voice for him to hear me."

The ladies nodded as they removed their needlework from their bags and Mr. Gilbert stared out the window.

Mrs. Gilbert shook her head. "See what I mean. And he won't let me check the battery or have it fixed. He tells me it will just start working on its own. Silly man! I'll send him over to collect the coffee," she said, leaving the counter to join her friends.

Georgie grabbed some mugs and set them on a tray. The bookshop included a simple café. Well, café was really stretching it. Behind the register, she had a coffee maker, doughnuts, and some homemade muffins. She'd dreamed of owning a store where patrons could enjoy browsing for books while sipping on a hot beverage or nibbling on a sweet treat. She'd hoped to expand the shop and build a dedicated space for it, along with a children's book section, once she had a little extra cash.

Becca handed her a plate of muffins when Mr. Gilbert ambled up with the help of his cane.

"Sounds like you should hear back soon," the man said with a sly twist to his lips.

Georgie set the items on the counter and stole a glance at the women, chatting while their needles dipped then emerged from their projects. "And I thought your hearing aid was out of commission."

"I'll take this over to the ladies," Becca said, grabbing the tray.

Mr. Gilbert leaned in and tapped the small, beige device in his ear. "It has a habit of going out whenever we get together with Marjorie's blue-haired brigade."

"You're terrible," Georgie said, but her smile told a different story.

Mr. and Mrs. Gilbert had been a staple of her clientele. Old friends of her grandparents, the Gilberts dropped by at least a couple times a week. And while Mr. Gilbert played the role of the old grumbler, he always carried Marjorie's purse, always held the door for her, and could often be caught gazing at her with a sentimental expression and the sweet hint of a smile.

"You're the dating expert, Georgie. You, better than anyone, should know the value of silence in a relationship," he countered, then gestured to the bulletin board on the wall, littered with layers of thank you letters and wedding photos of grateful Own the Eights believers who had followed her advice and found love with an eight.

She glanced at the board as a twinge of doubt twisted in her belly. But what about finding love herself? The truth was this; she was a dating expert who didn't have time to date. But she pushed the thought aside. She'd worry about that once her bills were paid.

"Okay, spill the deets, Georgie," Becca said, setting down the empty tray.

Georgie went back to twisting her apron tie. "From what I understand, they said that they'd notify the winner today. The CityBeat founders are running this themselves. They're an interesting pair—a little eccentric, and everything they do always seems to have a twist."

"But you've got to be a shoo-in for it, Georgie," Becca said, tossing a few muffin crumbs to Mr. Tuesday. "You've got a ton of followers, and people are stopping in all the time to tell you they found love following the Own the Eights protocol. I mean, my own sister met her husband using it!"

Mr. Gilbert chuckled. "Protocol? It still amazes me that it takes books and blogs and apps for you youngsters to find the one. Do you know how long it took me to fall for Marjorie?"

Georgie knew this story. When her grandparents were still

alive, and they'd get together with the Gilberts, after a glass of wine or two, Gene Gilbert often told the tale.

"Thirty seconds," he said, not waiting for her to answer. "She was the prettiest girl I'd ever seen. She had the sweetest laugh, and I just knew without even a word spoken between us that she'd be the one. And sixty-two years later, she still is."

Georgie patted the man's hand. "Unfortunately, Mr. Gilbert, you and Marjorie are not the norm. Most guys out there are real—"

"Places, ladies! Places!" one of the women called out.

"What's going on?" Georgie asked.

Mr. Gilbert chuckled. "I figured out why Marjorie's needlework group changed the time of their weekly meet-up at your shop."

Becca exchanged a knowing glance with Mr. Gilbert. "Yeah, it's pretty—"

"Pretty what? Have I missed something?" Georgie asked with a frown. If some kind of funny business was going on near her business, she needed to know about it.

"Oh, you've missed *something*, Georgie. You've missed it the last three weeks, taking Mr. Tuesday out for a walk in the alley behind the shop the last couple of times this happened," Becca added with a coy grin.

Georgie threw up her hands. "What happened? You're starting to worry me, Becca."

"Any minute, ladies!" a woman called with a giddy trill.

Mr. Gilbert glanced at his watch. "You'll see for yourself in about fifteen seconds."

Georgie scanned the front of the shop. All the women except for Marjorie were staring out the front window and onto the empty road.

"I don't know what you're talking about. I don't see anything that..." Georgie began, then froze as the *something* Becca had referenced passed by the window, and her brain clicked into slow-motion mode.

Like a framed moving portrait, a man's broad shoulders and shirtless, ripped torso appeared. Perfectly tanned skin wrapped his biceps and forearms, which looked damned near edible. If you were into that, not that she was, at all. Georgie tried to look away. Tried to think about anything other than muscles contracting and releasing as this Adonis of a man pumped his arms, driving forward on the pavement. A black hat sat on his head, pulled low, disguising his face, but not completely. A dark, perfectly groomed five o'clock shadow accompanied a strong jawline and the slope of a nose so perfect in its profile, plastic surgeons probably used this guy as a muse.

Her mouth grew dry. Her pulse kicked up. The air stilled as if she were trapped inside this moment, time, bending to lengthen an event only meant to last a few seconds.

"Georgie?" someone said, but she didn't quite have control of all her faculties yet.

Georgie blinked, and the figure blurred, speeding past the bookshop.

"Who was that?" she asked, staring out at the street.

"I think he works at that Deacon CrossFit that opened a few blocks from here. There's a bunch of them around the city. But, Georgie, you better check your phone," Becca instructed.

Georgie frowned, still feeling the aftershocks. "My what?"

An amused glint sparked in Mr. Gilbert's eyes. "Your phone. That thing all you kids can't stop looking at."

She shook her head. This was exactly what she warned women about, the guise of perfection. And she wasn't about to get carried away. Oh no! There was an excellent chance this guy was a perfect ten on the douchebag scale and not the lasting eight she preached about finding.

"What about my phone?"

Ping.

Georgie gasped. "It's beeping."

"That's what we've been trying to tell you," Mr. Gilbert said.

She snatched her phone from the counter. "This could be it!"

"Open it! Open it!" Becca cheered.

Georgie tapped the email icon, and her eyes went wide. "It's from them!"

"What does it say?" Becca asked, craning her head to try to get a look at the screen.

Georgie opened the email and scanned the message.

"Don't leave us in suspense," Mr. Gilbert prodded.

Her heart was beating a mile a minute.

"They want me to come in...today." She checked her watch. "In less than two hours to meet my teammates."

Becca scratched her head. "Why would you have teammates?"

Good question. But there had to be a reasonable answer.

Georgie gasped. "Possibly an editor or a producer. I think that once you get hired on with CityBeat, there's got to be a team you work with."

Becca nodded. "That makes sense. OMG, Georgie! You've got a team! What else does it say?"

She glanced back at the screen. "It says I'll get brought up to speed on the next steps in the meeting today."

"Next steps?" Becca mused, tapping the counter. "That's probably just ironing out your topics and timeline stuff, don't you think?"

Georgie nodded. "It has to be something like that."

But a pang of doubt rippled through her chest. She couldn't let herself get overly excited quite yet.

Mr. Gilbert patted her cheek. "You know, your dad would have been proud of you. Your grandparents, too. Are you going to tell your mom?"

That pang of doubt in her chest went from a ripple to a full swell at the mention of her mother. "Books and blogs aren't really her thing. I don't think she'd be very excited. I'm not quite the daughter she'd always wanted."

He gave her a sympathetic grin. "Just remember, Georgie, some of us have different ways of showing we care."

"Like faking a broken hearing aid?" she asked.

He chuckled. "If that means I get to feign ignorance to what the blue-haired brigade is jabbering on about and gaze at my wife like a lost puppy, then yes."

"You truly are an eight, Mr. Gilbert," she answered just as Becca's voice cut across the shop.

"Hey, ladies! Georgie got it! She won the contest!"

Applause broke out from the seating area, and Georgie gave them her best curtsey bow, then froze.

She had a lot to do!

"I have to go! I'm expected at CityBeat in less than two hours, and I need to walk Mr. Tuesday, drop him off at home, change my clothes, then get downtown."

"Don't you worry about the shop," Becca said, pressing her hands to her hips like she was ready to kick some bookshop ass. "I've got it covered, and I know Irene can help out anytime you need her."

"And I can take Mr. Tuesday for a walk," Mr. Gilbert offered.

Georgie patted her old friend's hand. "Thank you for offering, but I think a little walk would do me good. I need to get my thoughts in order and take a second to process everything."

At the mention of a walk, Mr. Tuesday procured his favorite slobbery ball from a basket of dog toys she kept behind the counter and began prancing at her feet.

"Wow," she said, shell-shocked as she removed her apron then plucked his leash from a wall hook.

"Way to go, kiddo," Mr. Gilbert added, before joining his wife and her needlework crew.

Becca shooed her toward the shop's back door. "Go! Go!"

Georgie left the shop, leaned against the back door to get her bearings, then wiped a tear from her cheek. "Lizzie, Hermione, Jane, we did it, ladies," she whispered to her imaginary trifecta, the three characters she loved so dearly. She'd lost count of how many times she'd reread *Pride and Prejudice*, *Jane Eyre*, and the *Harry Potter* series, and these characters had become as real to her as any friend, maybe better, because she knew them inside and out.

She released a sharp breath when a wave of nausea hit her.

What if they asked her why she hadn't found her eight? Her dear friend had married her eight, and she had thousands of emails from people who had found happiness using the Own the Eights method. Surely, that had to be enough.

But there was something else.

That email about meeting her teammates gnawed at her. The CityBeat founders were notorious for staging events and adding a surprising flair to anything they did.

But she'd won. Eccentric or not, they'd chosen her. This was her time to shine, and it had nothing to do with looks or weight or any shallow, superficial trait. Her mind. Her intelligence and her drive. That's what got her to this point.

She inhaled a cleansing breath, and just as she was about to blow it out, releasing all her anxious energy, a squirrel shot down the alleyway. She glanced at the leash in her hand. The leash she'd forgotten to attach to Mr. Tuesday's collar. And before she could even call out for him to stop, the squirrel chaser took off.

2

JORDAN

"Ninety-six, ninety-seven..."

"I can't do it, Jordan. I can't get to one hundred, man."

Jordan Marks easily held his push-up position and glanced at the young man next to him. Bird-like forearms shaking like rickety pipes and sweat streaming down his face, the guy struggled to lift himself back into a plank position.

"Look at me, Craig," Jordan said, his muscles strong and engaged as he maintained perfect form in his own plank.

The guy turned to him, red-faced and about to pass out.

But there was no way in hell Jordan was going to allow him to give up or let him collapse onto the floor of Deacon CrossFit.

"Craig, take a deep breath and focus."

The man complied, and the trembling subsided as a spark ignited in Jordan's chest.

This was what he lived for.

Pushing people to their physical and mental limits. Showing them that they deserved more and ingraining in their heads the Marks Perfect Ten Mindset's main principles: failure was not an option, finish what you start, and in every facet of your life, always be a ten.

The Marks Perfect Ten Mindset was his creation, his blog, that over the past two years, had thousands of followers, garnered millions of likes, and hopefully, if he got the news he expected to get today, his ticket to opening his own gym and jumpstarting his brand as not just the city's top personal trainer but to go global and spread the Marks Perfect Ten Mindset around the world.

Jordan hardened his features. "Tell me, Craig. Why are we here?"

"To get strong using the Marks Perfect Ten Mindset," the man bit out.

"What does that mean?" he barked.

"It means you try to be the best."

Jordan frowned. "Try?"

The man shook his head. "No, it means failure is not an option. It means you're never less than a perfect ten."

"Just in the gym?" Jordan prodded.

The man blew out a tight breath. "No, in every aspect of your life."

Hell yes! He had Craig right where he wanted him. The next step was to bring it home.

Jordan flicked his gaze to the mirror and caught a glimpse of his body and was rewarded with muscled perfection. Neat, styled hair—even in the gym—and a cocky smirk that said he had it all and knew it. Well, that's what he went out of his way to project.

He inhaled a slow even breath and went in for the kill, that satisfying moment when a client committed completely to the Marks Perfect Ten Mindset.

"All right, Craig. Stay with me."

The man nodded, drops of sweat falling to the mat.

Jordan held Craig's gaze. "There are two women on a bench. One has her hair in one of those God-awful messy buns. She's got glasses, baggy clothing, and those clunky sandals. The other is fit and rocking a miniskirt with fuck-me heels. She's got a killer body and looks that put a supermodel to shame. She's a total ten. Which woman do you ask out, Craig?"

The man gritted his teeth as determination burned in his eyes. "The ten."

"Damn right," he answered, cracking a triumphant grin.

Craig smiled through the pain as excitement surged through Jordan's veins.

Another Marks Perfect Ten Mindset convert. His program worked. He knew this from the thousands of before and after photos his clients and blog followers had sent him. But it never got old watching the shift and witnessing the moment when his client grabbed confidence by the reins and took off.

"You've got three more push-ups. Perfect ten push-ups. Come on! We'll do them together," he said, lowering himself an inch above the ground.

Craig powered through the final reps, and when they came to their feet, the entire gym cheered their success.

Craig beamed. "I did it!"

"Hell yeah. You owned it," Jordan answered, slapping the man's shoulder.

Craig wiped his face with a towel, grinning from ear to ear. "Thanks to you and the Marks Perfect Ten Mindset. Dude, I can't even imagine what it must be like to be you, *the* Jordan Marks. You've got it all. You've probably always had it all. It's nice of you to share a little bit of your awesomeness with us mere mortals."

Jordan grabbed his water bottle and took a long sip. That's precisely what he wanted everyone to think.

Jordan Marks, always a winner.

Jordan Marks, the specimen of physical perfection.

Jordan Marks, the guy who had it all.

He thought of the top drawer of his childhood dresser, and the muscles in his chest tightened.

Jordan Marks hadn't always been a perfect ten. Not even close—but that was his secret, his past, and he wasn't about to broadcast it to the world. The Marks Perfect Ten Mindset wasn't just his creation. It was also his shield, the barrier that stood between himself and a life best left forgotten.

He set the water bottle on a bench, brushed off the memories, and went back into badass trainer mode. "In the end, the Perfect Ten Mindset is a choice you have to make. I lay it out, but you have to do the work."

"Amen, brother!" Craig said, pride radiating off the guy in waves.

Jordan checked his watch. "That's it for today. Great work! Now, hit the shower."

Jordan grabbed his iPad to log in the training session when a sugary sweet voice, dripping with awe, cut through the hum of the treadmills, and the clang of free weights hitting the ground.

"Jordan, that was amazing!"

He didn't even turn around. He knew the buttered-up, baby doll sound of a gym bunny's coo and was well versed in the body language that said, this tiny scrap of a sports bra would look great on the floor of your bedroom, and so would I, buck naked, with your cock down my throat.

He'd had his share of gym pussy, one hell of a slice of it, especially when he was younger. But just shy of twenty-nine, he had bigger things on his mind than bending the gym's front desk receptionist over the leg press machine and fucking her hard and fast. He'd worked his ass off these past two years, training clients, opening new locations, and building his blog. And he didn't write *Dear Diary* bullshit posts either. Literal blood, sweat, and tears went into his articles. Hours of research went into deciding which protein powders to recommend. He spent his nights paging through sports medicine journals and his early mornings recording downloadable coached runs to share with his followers. He didn't have time for screwing around or screwing the cotton candy brained chicks who threw themselves at him in droves.

Sure, he could have his pick of women. But his sights were set on the Marks Perfect Ten Mindset becoming a household name, and himself, a leader in healthy life transformations.

He'd show all those fuckers from his past that he'd won. That he was better than them in every single aspect that mattered, appearance and success.

"That's why we keep him around."

A smile pulled at the corners of his mouth. Now, this was a voice worth acknowledging.

Jordan glanced up from his iPad to find the sturdy frame of Deacon Perry, the founder of the Deacon CrossFit chain, striding toward him. Gray flecks threaded through the man's dark hair as he surveyed the gym.

Jordan shook the man's hand. "It's good to see you, Deacon."

"The place looks great. Any hiccups?"

"This is the fifth location I've opened for you, Deac. I've got it covered."

The man gave him an approving nod. "Only open three months and already running like a well-oiled machine."

"Jordan's the bomb. We've even had professional athletes calling to schedule sessions with him," came the syrupy voice of the desk receptionist, Shelly.

He turned to the young woman. She fit the bill for the look Deacon wanted for his CrossFit front desk staff. Young, perky, and trim, Shelly was the first thing clients saw when they entered. And she wasn't just a pretty face. She'd already worked the desk at a few rec centers in the city, and more importantly, he'd never hire an idiot. But she was still a woman, and it wasn't her fault she couldn't help falling all over herself around him.

Most women did.

Jordan hardened his features and met the woman's gaze. He was all for praise and admiration. He lived for the likes he received on his posts and loved seeing his subscriber numbers rise, but he needed to talk to Deacon and didn't have time for Shelly and her effusive adoration.

"Some boxes got delivered this morning, Shelly. Can you go through them? It should be the promotional giveaway prizes for our new clients."

"Anything for you, Jordan," she answered with a swish of her ponytail.

"Are you tapping that?" Deacon asked under his breath as Shelly jogged to the front.

Jordan shook his head. "No, man. You know I keep it professional."

Deacon's gaze hovered over Shelly's Lycra covered ass. "I may need to stop in here more often."

"She's twenty-two, Deac."

"My favorite number," the man answered without missing a beat.

Jordan shifted his weight. "I did want to talk to you about something I've got coming up. Do you have a minute?"

"Yeah, I've got some time," the man answered with a curious expression.

His mentor knew something was up.

Jordan steadied himself. Jordan Marks didn't get nervous. Jordan Marks owned the room, any room. Six four and built like a god with a face to match, jittery was not a word in his vocabulary. At least, that's what he tried to project. But today could be a game changer, and the butterflies in his stomach agreed.

"Let's talk in the back," he offered.

Deacon followed him, past a row of state-of-the-art cardio machines and several trainers working with clients, to a small office tucked near the locker rooms.

Deacon settled himself in a chair as Jordan sat behind the desk.

"Now, spill, Marks. I've known you long before you became Marks Perfect whatever. What's going on?"

"You do read my emails?" Jordan quipped.

Deacon stretched his arms then relaxed into the seat. "In between the ones sent from Maureen's lawyers."

Jordan leaned forward. "About the divorce?"

It seemed crazy that Deacon and his wife were splitting up. He'd known Deac's wife, Maureen, as long as he'd known his mentor, and she'd been like a second mother to him. She'd given up her teaching career to help get Deacon CrossFit off the ground and now devoted herself to raising their girls.

The man sighed. "Divorce. Time with the kids. The amount of spousal support. It's always something. Now, come on, Jordan. Tell me what's on your mind."

He'd met Deacon a decade ago entirely by chance. Working at a deli as a delivery guy in college, he'd been sent to Deacon CrossFit to drop off some sandwiches. Rail thin and gangly, he wasn't surprised when he'd entered the gym, and a couple of bulked-up meatheads started giving him shit.

Careful with that bag, Tinker Bell. It looks pretty heavy for you.

He'd heard it all and was just about to brush off another bout of bullying when Deacon Perry strode up to the front with an air of confidence, that at the time, Jordan never even dreamed of attaining. The hulk of a man looked him up and down, then made him an offer.

You want to make sure no one ever fucks with you again? Come back tomorrow.

And he did just that. He showed up the next day and the day after that.

Every day for the next four years.

His time in Deacon's gym transformed his life. He graduated from college with a double major in English Literature and Kinesiology and Exercise Science, and Deac was right. He'd put on fifty pounds of muscle, ran a six-minute mile, and could bench press three-fifty in his sleep—and nobody fucked with him. Through damn hard work and dedication, the skinny kid from the Colorado plains stepped foot into Deacon's gym a lamb and came out a lion.

Jordan brought up the gym's master calendar on the computer and tilted the screen for Deacon to see. "I've rearranged the schedule for the next three weeks."

Deacon slipped on a pair of glasses from his pocket and gazed at the screen. "I don't see you on there very much."

"I did that on purpose. You see, Deac, I've entered a contest, and if I win, I'll need the next few weeks to focus on my blog."

"That perfect thing?" his mentor asked, raising an eyebrow.

"Yes, the Marks Perfect Ten Mindset."

Deacon sat back and pocketed his glasses. "What kind of contest is this?"

"If I win it, I'll become a paid contributor on the CityBeat site."

Deacon whistled. "Even I know of CityBeat. They've got a huge fitness community."

Jordan nodded. "It's a complete lifestyle platform, and if I get it, things could really pick up for me."

Deacon narrowed his gaze. "I see. And Deacon CrossFit? Is that a part of your plan?"

A twist of regret gripped his heart. "I owe you everything, Deac. I'd never leave you hanging. But this could be big for me."

"And you're pretty sure you've won?" the man asked.

Jordan crossed his arms. "I can't see how they'd choose anyone else. There are only a few other blogs that come close to my number of subscribers, and one is a bullshit relationship wannabe guru. There are a few other lifestyle bloggers, but, as far as content, I'm clearly the best."

His mentor looked him square in the eyes. "You do what you need to do to win, son."

Son.

The word shouldn't still sting, but it did.

"When do you find out?" Deacon pressed.

Jordan glanced at his phone, laying on the desk. "Today, I'm just waiting on an email."

"I can tell," Deacon answered, biting back a grin.

Jordan frowned. "What do you mean?"

"Look at your leg."

Bouncing up and down like a tween waiting to meet Justin Bieber, his knee bobbed with nervous energy. He forced it to stop. He needed to get his shit under control.

He came to his feet. "That's nothing. This is when I usually hit the pavement for a quick afternoon 5K."

Deacon's lips twisted into a wry grin. "You might want to make it a ten today."

Jordan nodded. "I probably should, and thanks for backing me on this. You know I won't let you down with the gym."

Deacon watched him closely. "Just know who got you to this point."

"I know, Deac, and I'm so grateful to you and," he stopped himself, nearly mentioning Maureen.

A muscle twitched in his mentor's jaw. "Damn right! You've come a long way from—"

"Straws!" came a shrill, sugary voice, and Jordan froze.

He could almost hear the taunts and see the kids' laughing faces.

Straws. Fucking straws. Pelting him in the head. Brushing past his skinny limbs.

"Why the hell would you say that?" he barked at Shelly, who froze like a deer caught in a pair of headlights.

The girl crumpled. "Because I opened the boxes in the front with the water bottles, and I thought the smaller box with the straws for them was in here?"

He swallowed hard, then found the box on the floor by the door. "Yeah, this is probably it," he said, handing it to her.

Shelly skittered away without a swish to her ponytail this time.

"Walk me out," Deacon said, eyeing Shelly's ass again as she left the office.

Jordan grabbed a ball cap, swiped his phone and earbuds off the desk, and followed his mentor out of the gym.

Once on the pavement, Deacon put a hand on his shoulder. "Who taught you how to be the best, Jordan?"

A wave of resolve crashed over him, washing away the vexing memories.

He was not the skinniest kid in his class. He was *the* Jordan Marks.

"You did, Deac," he answered, his voice steady.

"Now, get that run in, clear your head, and prepare for success."

"Thanks," he said to the man who'd been more of a father to him than his real father had ever been.

"And Jordan?"

"Yeah, Deac."

"What do you know about Shelly?"

He shrugged. "She works the desk."

Deacon nodded and glanced inside the gym. "Go crush that 10K!" he said, his gaze trained on the front desk.

Jordan bit back a grin. Jesus! What was Deac thinking? But

he had bigger things to worry about than his mentor checking out a pretty girl. He popped in his earbuds, set off down the street, then glanced at his phone. He'd get in his run, and then he'd check his email—because discipline mattered. Yes, he wanted the CityBeat gig. He wanted fame and notoriety.

But he was not a quitter.

If he set a goal, he exceeded it. He told himself he'd run three miles today. Instead, he'd follow Deac's advice and run six. Pushing his body to the limit with each stride, he stripped off his shirt and tucked it in the band of his mesh shorts as he passed by the shops and cafés dotting the Tennyson town center.

He liked this neighborhood and had rented a small bungalow not far from the gym. Working for Deacon, he'd been all over the state setting up CrossFit locations. But this place, while still near the bustling city, had a small-town feel to it that strangely appealed to him. He kicked up his pace, darting off the sidewalk and onto the road to pass a couple pushing a stroller. He cut back onto the pavement and passed a little bookshop, that lately, seemed to be packed with old ladies staring out of the front window.

He regulated his breathing, his body grateful to burn off the nervous energy he'd harbored all day. He crossed the street and headed for a large patch of open space. He'd finish his run at Tennyson Park, doing laps under the shade of the giant oaks and beech trees that lined a trail circling the space. He'd completed twelve laps when his phone beeped, signaling the six-mile mark. And like a kid waiting to go downstairs on Christmas morning, anticipation building, he stopped and stared at the email icon on his screen.

"CityBeat is yours," he whispered, then pressed the envelope icon.

One new message.

Subject: Congratulations from CityBeat.

He scanned the message. Show up today. Meet the team.

Fuck yes!

He was going to be big, bigger than big. Big enough to show everyone that he wasn't a scrawny kid without a backbone.

He was Jordan Marks of the Marks Perfect Ten Mindset.

He started to type a reply when a shouting woman caught his attention.

"Grab him!" she called.

He looked around, but before he could make out if she were talking to him, a small blur of brown fuzz zoomed past him, followed by a larger blur of barking black and white fur.

And then, her.

Sprinting in those clunky Birkenstock sandals, a terrible choice for running, was a woman with a dark tangle of hair, twisted into a bun on the top of her head. Tendrils framed her face as she made her way closer. Her running form was complete shit, but he couldn't look away. He couldn't help but notice the curve of her neck and the sway of her hips. Clad in a cardigan that completely clashed with her skirt, she was mesmerizing. If he needed an example of the opposite of a Marks Perfect Ten Mindset woman, she'd be it.

He blinked.

It had to be the complete train wreck aspect of her appearance that had him enthralled.

She skidded to a stop in front of him with a dog leash clutched in her hand and gasped.

"It's you!" she said, eyes as wide as saucers.

"Me?" he asked, giving her a pleasant enough smile.

He shouldn't be surprised. Ripped torso and shoulders that would put a linebacker to shame, he often left women stunned. And, as his blog popularity had grown, more people around the city had started to recognize him. But there was something in her expression that surprised him. A thread of derision he wasn't used to, or at least, hadn't experienced in a long time.

She studied his face. "You have a dimple."

"Yeah?" he answered, smile fading.

Who the fuck was this? She certainly wasn't anyone he'd ever crossed paths with—or had he? He'd seen her somewhere.

"Brice Casey," she said under her breath, venom lacing each syllable.

It was his turn to study her. "No, sorry, that's not me."

She shook her head as if she were shaking off a memory. "Can you help me catch my dog? I think we can cut him off. There's a fence, so he's got to come back this way after he's done chasing that damn squirrel."

Jordan glanced at his watch. Shit! He was cutting it close as it was.

He needed to get back to the gym and make sure one of the other trainers could close up, then get home and grab a quick shower before heading downtown to the CityBeat offices.

The breathless woman threw up her hands. "Hey, shirtless man! Woman in need! Can. You. Help."

He met her gaze. Women didn't talk to him like this.

"Yeah, I just...I have a thing to get to," he stammered.

He didn't fucking stammer.

She huffed out an audible breath. "So do I. A life-changing thing. But I have to catch my dog first. Can you help me for two minutes?"

He glanced at the animal, running from tree to tree. "What's its name?"

"*His* name is Mr. Tuesday," she answered.

He reared back. "What kind of name is that?"

She pressed her hands to her hips. "The name he had when I adopted him from the shelter."

"You could have changed it," he countered.

"Well, I didn't!" She narrowed her gaze. "Are you always this unpleasant?"

Unpleasant?

No woman had ever called him *unpleasant*. And she seemed to be completely unaware that she was near eye to eye with his sculpted chest and carved abs. That alone should have had her biting her lip and gazing at him through batted eyelashes.

But not this bohemian, cardigan crusader with a pair of glasses hanging on a chain around her neck.

"I don't even know you, lady."

"Thank God for that," she huffed.

He bent forward. "Hey, messy bun girl, you need my help. How about a little gratitude?"

She gasped. "Did you just call me, messy bun girl?"

He raised an eyebrow. "You've got one, right?"

She reached up and tucked a strand of hair behind her ear, and he flexed his hands.

Did he want to be the one brushing her chocolate brown locks from trailing across her face?

Jesus! Hell no, he didn't.

What was wrong with him?

"Well, yeah, I guess I do have a messy bun," she answered without quite as much spite.

He gestured toward the leash. "And by the way, I don't own any pets, but I'm pretty sure those things work better when you actually attach them to your animal."

"Such a Brice Casey," she mumbled.

"Who the hell is this Brice guy?"

Jesus! Did he miss some hipster pop culture reference?

She shook her head, glanced at her dog, currently running circles around an old oak, and softened her expression. "It doesn't matter. Can you just help me?"

When she wasn't yelling or glaring at him, she was kind of...

STOP!

He gestured with his chin. "You go left. I'll go right."

She pressed her hand to her chest, bringing his attention to what almost looked like a really nice pair of tits hidden under that dreadful cardigan, and let out a sweet little sigh. "Okay! Thank you! I'm sorry for calling you unpleasant. I'm a little out of sorts today."

She had lovely eyes. Not quite blue and not quite green, and they sparkled like gemstones.

He flicked his gaze to her shoes. He had to quash these thoughts. There was too damned much on the line. "Try not to twist your ankle running in those poor excuse for sandals."

She frowned, probably about to take back her apology, when the dog caught sight of a rabbit and bolted.

"Oh no!" she cried, and he knew he had to act if he wanted to catch that dog and make it to CityBeat on time.

He wasn't quite as fast as a dog in pursuit of a floppy-eared animal, but he was fast enough. With messy bun girl trailing behind him, calling out the dog's stupid name, he swooped in behind the mutt and grabbed its collar, but lost his footing and skidded to the ground with the dog landing on top of him, panting wildly. The mongrel looked down at him and licked his face.

Oh, for fuck's sake!

The last thing that dog probably licked was his balls.

This was so not a Marks Perfect Ten situation.

"He likes you," messy bun girl cooed, coming to her knees and scratching between the dog's ears.

"Do you mind?" he asked, gaze bouncing from the ground to the dog.

She pressed her hand to her chest again. "Sorry! Come on, Mr. Tuesday. Let's let the man get up."

She looked up at him, still on the ground, cradling her dog's head in her hands. "Thank you, Mr...."

Warmth spread through his chest as he watched her press a kiss to the top of the dog's head, but he pushed the feeling aside. Nothing about her or her harebrained dog fit his life's motto.

He sharpened his expression. "You can call me, Mr. Use-Your-Damn-Leash-Next-Time. You're not the only person with things to do today."

She scoffed as contempt replaced the kindness in her eyes. "If I weren't a nice person, I'd call you a supreme asshat."

He gave her his best shit-eating grin. "Well, this asshat is probably going to be late, thanks to you."

"Such a Brice Casey," she murmured, repeating that bizarre hipster reference again as he doubled his pace and set off toward the gym.

3

GEORGIE

Georgie glanced at the clock on the dashboard of her compact Volkswagen Rabbit. "You won't be late. You won't be late. You won't be late."

She might be late.

Thanks to Mr. Tuesday, and no thanks to Mr. Park Jerk, aka Brice Casey-esque creep, she'd barely had time to get Mr. Tuesday home and settled. She managed to pull a comb through her hair and quickly redo her bun. There was no way she was going to let her thick locks loose without a real wash and a blowout, which she had no time for due to the squabbling and garden variety asshattery she'd endured from that guy who'd barely agreed to help her.

The nerve! Talk about zero humanity.

All Brice Casey and no Mr. Darcy, and her literary trifecta agreed. Well, they almost agreed. They tried to remind her that first impressions often didn't tell the whole story. But Georgie was a master in sussing out the Brice Casey type. She'd written a myriad of posts on it.

But what cut her to the core was that she'd almost abandoned her Own the Eights principles when the asshat turned out to be the same guy who'd left her all googly-eyed when he'd run past her bookshop. She'd nearly slipped when she called out for help and met his piercing green eyes and really got a look at his torso that would never need photoshop. It had taken all her restraint not to run her fingers down the hard plane of his abdomen just to make sure he was real.

His body was so perfect it nearly took her breath away—for the second time that day. Until his perfection and craptastic demeanor snapped her back. Yet, he had helped her. He'd caught Mr. Tuesday. He'd been a complete jerk about it, but he'd done it.

Ah! Forget about him!

Her car sputtered and whined, the gears grinding together, something else she'd need to use her winnings to take care of, as she parked in front of the CityBeat building, grateful to find a spot. She cut the ignition, closed her eyes, and took two cleansing breaths. Meandering walks and meditation were vital components of the Own the Eights philosophy. She had no time to meander, so it was up to meditation to quickly clear her mind and open the channels of positive energy. She'd just interviewed a local yoga teacher for the blog a few weeks ago and had written about using meditation to curb initial superficial attraction. It was a huge hit, garnering thousands of likes.

She inhaled then exhaled, emptying her thoughts of perfection and surface-level attraction.

That's all it had been today. In a moment of panic, her thoughts racing, she'd fallen under the shirtless man's spell. Totally reasonable under the circumstances. And so what if he worked in the area. She'd stay in her neck of the woods, tucked away in her little bookshop, and he could reign supreme over his Perfectville in some hyper-masculine gym, pumping iron and roid-raging his nuts into raisins.

That's a good one.

Georgie smiled. It was always quite a compliment when Lizzie Bennet liked something she came up with.

With one last cleansing breath, she grabbed her bag and a folder with all her blog post ideas. She'd submitted several to CityBeat already but wanted to be ready to address her team if they needed more ideas.

Team!

She was nearly bursting with excitement. Surely, they'd have to be like-minded people—total Own the Eights converts. Why would CityBeat make them her team if they weren't?

And the possibilities to expand Own the Eights were endless. From more in-depth dating advice to healthy living to environmentally friendly practices to volunteering to help the community, there were so many avenues they could pursue, so many fruitful, soul-satisfying ways to help people connect with their eight.

She entered the CityBeat building and headed for the reception desk and caught her reflection in one of the mirrored panels. No, she hadn't had time to change her clothes. But this was who she was, a pattern mixing, bookshop owning, advice-giving, crusader for authentic, meaningful connection, who just happened to love Birkenstocks and cardigans. She studied her reflection, pleased she hadn't fallen prey to altering her wardrobe to impress some shallow Brice Casey-like bottom-dweller when she collided into a wall.

Not a wall.

A back.

And not any back.

His back.

Even with a shirt on, she recognized the broad shoulders and the punishingly perfect cut of his muscled forearms.

He turned and gripped her elbow, which would have been a

very chivalrous gesture if he hadn't immediately cringed when they made eye contact.

"Are you following me?" He scoffed.

She gasped. "Am I following you?"

He shook his head. "Yeah, that's what I just asked you. Did you lose your dog again?"

"No, Mr. Use-Your-Damn-Leash. That is what you said your name was, correct? I am not following you." She reared back and pressed her hand to her chest. "Oh, my God! Are you following me?"

His jaw dropped. "Why would I follow you?"

"You're here, aren't you?" she shot back.

Incredulity marred his perfect features. "Yeah, I got here first. You got here second. Any kindergartner could tell you that means you're following me."

She held his gaze, willing her retinas to acquire laser power to blast this asshat off the planet.

"Miss Jensen?" a woman said, cutting through the tension.

Georgie blinked. "Yes, that's me."

"I thought so. You and Mr. Marks are expected upstairs. Mr. Garcia and Mr. Chang are waiting for you on the twelfth floor," the woman said serenely as if there was nothing odd about two strangers verbally assaulting each other in the CityBeat lobby.

Georgie cocked her head to the side. "Hector Garcia and Bobby Chang, CityBeat's founders, are waiting for the two of us? Me and him?" she added, pointing back and forth.

"Wow, you are speedy-quick on the uptake, lady," this *Mr. Marks* said under his breath.

She flicked her gaze from the receptionist over to the creep. "You, sir, are one supreme asshat."

"I guess you're not nice," he replied with a smirk.

Georgie jerked her head back. "I am nice. I volunteer at animal shelters."

He shrugged. "I remember you saying just a few hours ago that if you weren't a nice person, you'd call me a supreme asshat."

"If the shoe fits," she mumbled, taking a page from his playbook.

He glanced down at her feet. "I should probably use my supreme asshat status to let you know that seventeen BC is calling, and they'd like their sandals back."

"These are Birkenstocks," she bit out in a tight whisper.

They were comfortable and supported her high arches. If she controlled the universe, she'd decree them the eighth wonder of the world.

"Yep, and they still belong in the dark ages," he replied, crossing his arms.

Unable to reply—because what kind of creep could have beef with comfortable footwear—Georgie stood stock still in a dazed stupor. Thankfully, the receptionist pulled her out of her state of utter shock when she came around from behind the desk and handed them name badges.

"Jordan Marks and Georgie Jensen, here you go. The elevators are to your left. Once you're on the twelfth floor, take a right. You can't miss Mr. Garcia and Mr. Chang's office."

Georgie turned to the woman and lowered her voice. "Are you sure he's supposed to be here?"

"I'm literally standing next to you. I can hear everything you just said," the asshat, Jordan, said and shook his head.

"Yes, you're both supposed to be here," the woman answered.

Georgie nodded then clipped her name badge to her cardigan as Jordan did the same, minus the cardigan. If she wasn't so well versed in her Own the Eights methodology, she might have noticed that he was wearing the hell out of a button-up shirt with the sleeves rolled casually, exposing his forearms.

She sighed. And what forearms they were.

Hermione, Jane, and Lizzie held up blaring air horns, shocking her out of her forearm stupor and signaling for her to hightail it to the elevator. Unfortunately, Jordan Marks, God, what a stupid name, followed her into the tight space and pressed the button for the twelfth floor.

She caught him checking out her reflection in the mirrored elevator and met his gaze. "This is a big day for me. I'm not sure what business you have with the CityBeat founders, but I'm here for a very important reason," she said, looking into the eyes of his stupid perfect reflection.

"Yeah, me too. Can we just agree to keep out of each other's way? You do what you need to do, and I'll take care of my business. Deal?" he asked her reflection.

"Fine, deal," she said, turning to him and extending her hand.

"You want to shake on it?" he asked.

"Yeah, it needs to be a real deal," she sneered. She rarely sneered. It was such an unpleasant expression, but this seemed like the right time to do it.

He reached out and took her hand into his, and his touch knocked the sneer clean off her face. The breath caught in her throat, and heat pulsed from his body into hers as her heart rate skyrocketed. Butterflies erupted in her belly, and her mouth grew dry just like when she'd seen him run past the bookshop.

She looked up, and he stared at her with a dumbfounded expression. There was no handshaking going on, only hand-holding, and she hadn't held anyone's hand in...

She could barely remember.

It had to have been before the Brice Casey incident. She'd gone to the movies with a guy she'd met online, and he'd held her hand. But he did it after he'd wolfed down ninety-nine percent of the buttery popcorn, which made for a slimy grip. Holding Jordan's hand had to be the polar opposite of that slippery experience. His hands were warm and just the right amount of rough, probably from gripping weights or throwing boulders or whatever musclebound morons did to get a body like his.

Ripped abs.

Sculpted arms.

Even his legs were perfect.

Perfect!

She gasped as the elevator pinged their arrival to the twelfth floor and pulled her hand from his grip.

"It's a deal," she murmured, darting between the barely open elevator doors.

Holy Mary! Touching him was...a momentary lapse in judgment, right?

But her trifecta wasn't buying it. She could picture their skeptical expressions. It was time to bring out the big guns, aka her list. Her Own the Eights list. She needed to fall back on the advice she gave her followers every day. Think of the list and remember that good looks and great hair were scribbled out in permanent ink. She glanced over her shoulder at Jordan, a few paces behind her.

He had great hair. Short, but not too short. His jet-black locks with just the hint of a curl were coiffed to perfection along with his five o'clock shadow, which often looked messy on most men, but really worked for him.

"Gah! Stop!" she mumbled.

"Yes, stop. We're here," he said with a grating edge to his voice.

She turned to find Jordan standing by a door with the founders' names stenciled into the frosted glass.

"Oh, right. I was kind of in my head."

"And mumbling like a crazy lady," he said, opening the door for her and found what looked like an adult Chuck E. Cheese.

Hanging swings and retro arcade machines dotted the space, while ping-pong tables and a bank of television and computer screens lined the walls. Sofas and futons created little enclaves of comfortable workspace. The office, if that's what you'd call it, had to be double or triple the square footage of her entire house.

"Look, Bobby!" a man exclaimed. "It's Own the Eights gal and the Marks Perfect Ten Mindset guy! Our first team has arrived!"

Team?

But before she could give that whopper another thought, she was eye to eye with Hector Garcia and Bobby Chang. She'd know these two men anywhere. Their faces were splashed all over the CityBeat website. Hector and Bobby were the tech power couple who started the Colorado-based company. Originally a site for metro Denver lifestyle blogging, CityBeat had exploded to become the most trusted and visited place on the web to get the pulse of a city, just about any city on every continent, even Antarctica, where a Norwegian scientist stationed there blogs about the pitfalls of falling in love with a penguin researcher. Spoiler, this penguin researcher wanted the scientist to wear flippers when they were getting it on. Truly, a captivating and somewhat disturbing blog, to say the least.

Bobby fiddled with his glasses before giving them an awkward nod. Hector was the flashy, flamboyant partner, a tech genius in his own right, but it was rumored his husband, the quieter Bobby, was the real brains behind the CityBeat platform. Together, they'd taken over the blogging world as the premiere lifestyle blogging destination.

"Let's sit," Hector said, gesturing to two small couches positioned across from one another. Hector and Bobby settled themselves on one side as she reluctantly sat down next to Jordan, who'd turned a ghostly shade of dishwater gray.

"Alana called up and told us you two met in the lobby," Hector said with a wide grin.

"Alana?" she asked.

"The receptionist who gave you your badges," Bobby answered.

"You each thought you'd won, didn't you?" Hector asked with a glint in his eye.

She shared a look with Jordan. "Yeah, I thought I'd won."

"I did as well," Jordan answered, his voice void of cocky bravado.

Hector rubbed his hands together. "Let's just say, you've made it to the final round of competition, and now we're going to see what you're really made of."

"We're competing against each other?" Jordan asked.

"Yes and no. You're going to be working together," Hector said, opening a folder on the table and handing them each a piece of paper. "This is a loose schedule. We still want you to maintain your blogs and keep doing what you're doing. But we're adding in some surprise events—challenges—that could be sprung on you at any time. Luckily, you both live and work in the same area, Jordan at the Deacon CrossFit and Georgie at Jensen's Books. That'll be convenient."

"But I thought there was going to be just one winner," Jordan posited.

Bobby and Hector shared a curious look. "Yes, we want to shake things up around here with some fresh talent."

"Then how will you decide?" she asked.

"Likes," Bobby answered.

"Likes?" she parroted back.

Bobby pushed his glasses up from where they'd slid down his nose. "Yes, you'll each post about your experience on the challenges you complete together, and we'll use the likes metric to calculate your scores."

Jordan crossed his arms. "But our blogs are completely different."

"Not really," Bobby countered gently. "If you boil your blogs down to the basics, they're actually quite similar."

Georgie sat forward. "I need to respectfully disagree, Mr. Chang. Own the Eights has nothing in common with the Marks Perfect Ten Mindset."

She'd seen posts from Jordan's blog pop up in her newsfeed. With titles like *Pick a Perfect Protein Powder* and *How to Date a Ten*, there was no way they were alike.

Hector offered the hint of a smile. "You both offer ways to better oneself, correct?"

"And you both give relationship, lifestyle, and fitness advice," Bobby added.

Jordan put up his hand. "I need to agree with Georgie and respectfully disagree. What kind of fitness advice could Georgie dispense? You just said that she works at a bookstore."

She lifted her chin. "I *own* a bookstore."

Jordan waved off the comment. "Fine, but still. What kind of exercise advice are you qualified to blog about?"

She gave him her best shit-eating grin. "Meditation, yoga, and meandering walks."

"Meandering what?" Jordan questioned.

"Walks," she repeated as if she were addressing an idiot—because she was. "Meandering walks are an excellent way to not only get in a little exercise but also an outlet to spark creativity and fresh ideas."

He smirked. "Did you come up with that outfit combination on a *meandering* walk?"

She channeled the take-no-shit attitude of Hermione Granger and gave him her best stink eye. "Did I call you a supreme asshat on the way up here? I should have called you,

His Majesty the High Emperor of Asshattery. What an honor it is to bask in your eternal perfection."

She held his burning gaze, unwavering.

"This is going to be great!" Hector cooed, cutting short their staring contest.

"Great?" she and her asshat partner snapped in unison.

Hector nodded. "The energy between the two of you is electric! The CityBeat readers will love it."

She blushed. The Emperor of Asshattery name-calling was not professional, but the CityBeat founders seemed to love it.

Hector leaned in. "Listen, you both are very comfortable in your worlds. Putting you together may shake things up for both your blogs, in a good way."

"And you do share many crossover followers," Bobby added.

"What are those?" she asked.

Bobby picked up an iPad from the table and tapped a few icons. "See, sixty-nine percent of your followers are the same. Georgie, while you started out with a mostly female following, you've been steadily adding men. And Jordan, you're just the opposite. You started with a predominantly male following and have taken on quite a few female subscribers."

"Hold on!" Jordan exclaimed. "Sixty-nine percent of my followers also follow the Own the Eights blog?"

"Numbers don't lie," Bobby answered, showing them a screen packed with data and metrics.

Georgie sat back, grateful for the overstuffed cushion currently keeping her upright. How could that be? How could her loyal Own the Eights followers also subscribe to a blog as shallow and vapid as the Marks Perfect Ten Mindset?

"They just do," Hector answered, biting back a grin.

Mortified, she glanced around the room. "Did I just say that aloud?"

"Every vapid word," Jordan shot back. The color had

returned to his face, now with a slightly pink hue to his perfect cheekbones.

"So, that's it? Georgie and I complete a series of challenges together for the next few weeks?" Jordan asked.

It wasn't going to be pleasant, but she'd endured worse. Way worse. And she knew her blog and understood her followers. They'd be behind her all the way, wouldn't they? Or would they back Jordan?

"Not quite. We do have a little twist up our sleeves," Hector answered, a curious glint in his eyes as the opaque doors to the office opened and in walked the life-sized version of Barbie and Ken.

If Jordan was perfection, these individuals were perfection version 2.0.

Hector waved the pair over. "This, Georgie and Jordan, is your competition."

Holy hell! The Dannies from the DannyLyfe blog had arrived.

Yes, that's *life* spelled with a *Y. L-y-f-e.*

Jordan hardened his features. While Georgie's blog, with her meandering walks and rah-rah, girl power posts were mind-numbing—a few had popped up in his newsfeed, and he may have read one or two—the Dannies were exponentially worse. A brother and sister team, Daniel and Danielle, who blogged on the site and preached pseudoscience and pushed their own line of supplements, the Dannies were not only reckless, they were dangerous.

And unfortunately, they were all over CityBeat, racking up almost one hundred thousand followers more than he had.

"Sorry, we're late. We just finished running a marathon," Danielle said with every blond hair on her head perfectly in place.

A muscle ticked in his jaw. He wasn't about to kowtow to these two. The blond-haired blue-eyed duo spouted healthy living and relationship tips, but everything about them screamed plastic. From her have-to-be-fake tits to his obvious calf implants to their Botox fresh faces, there was no way their healthy glow came from anything other than one hell of a chemical peel.

"I hadn't heard of any marathons scheduled in the city today," he remarked coolly.

Daniel met his gaze. "It wasn't a race. That's just our level of commitment to fitness. Our followers appreciate our dedication."

"And then there was the kitten," Danielle added, swishing her blond ponytail over her shoulder.

"What about a kitten?" Georgie asked.

Ah shit! He couldn't have Georgie falling under the Dannies' spell.

As if on cue, one tear trailed down Danielle's cheek. "It was in the middle of the road about to be decimated by a truck when Daniel sprinted into traffic and rescued it."

"Oh, thank goodness!" Georgie replied. He glanced over at her. Was she about to cry?

"And then we had to take the little guy to a vet to make sure he was okay," Daniel continued.

Georgie gasped. "And was he all right?"

Danielle pressed her hands together as if she were giving thanks or trying to show off her perfectly manicured nails, probably the latter. "Yes! Completely healthy, and we were able to find the sweet thing a wonderful home with a loving family who just happens to be loyal DannyLyfe subscribers."

Georgie's eyes went wide. "You did all that before coming here today?"

"Well, of course, we worked in the garden then donated the organic produce to a homeless shelter before we left on our run," Danielle answered, then glanced at her brother. "Kind of a light day for us."

"Danielle and Daniel, meet Georgie Jensen and Jordan

Marks," Hector said, gesturing for the Dannies to join them on the couch.

"You'll be competing against each other to see who wins the contest to become a CityBeat contributor," Bobby added.

"A competition?" Daniel echoed.

Hector handed the Dannies a schedule. "While your blog has the most followers, we wanted to add a little twist to City-Beat's Battle of the Blogs, that's what we're calling it now, and give two other bloggers a chance to compete. Jordan and Georgie blog separately but will be working together during the competition period. Since you two are a team, we didn't think it fair for Georgie and Jordan to be alone."

Agitation surged through his body. *Fair*? How could Hector and Bobby not see that tethering him to Georgie wasn't giving him an advantage at all? He'd be better off on his own.

But that wasn't an option.

Danielle's serene expression cracked. "If they're working together, how will you decide who wins? And, you're still offering the ten-thousand-dollar prize money, right?" she tagged on a bit too sweetly.

Bobby shared a quick, inquisitive glance with Hector then nodded. "Yes, the winner will still receive the prize money, and we have a two-tiered scoring apparatus in place. Georgie and Jordan's likes will be combined since the two of them together have about as many followers as you and your brother do on the DannyLyfe blog. If you're ahead, then you win. If Georgie and Jordan are ahead, we'll determine the winner by which one of them individually garnered the most likes."

The Dannies shared a glance, their eyeballs bouncing up and down as if they were speaking some silent retinal language. With all the work it looked like they'd had done, he wouldn't be surprised if they had transmitters implanted in their brains.

"I see," Daniel answered, sharing an uneasy expression with his sibling.

"Not to worry! Daniel and I are always up for some good clean competition," Danielle added as she turned up the wattage on her grin.

Hector shared another curious look with Bobby then clapped his hands. "Excellent! Now, all of you have signed the contract to compete. But I wanted to remind you that, at any time, CityBeat could send media to film or photograph you. We're sinking quite a bit of advertising dollars into promoting the competition, and you'll need to be ready for anything."

Shit!

How the hell was the poster girl for cardigans supposed to help him, the Marks Perfect Ten Mindset creator, expand his brand and compete on a level with the Dannies? And be recorded doing it?

He silenced his internal rant and thought of Deacon.

Who taught you to be the best?

What would Deac do? He'd fucking kill it. He wouldn't let any obstacle get in his way of victory, and neither would Jordan Marks.

He was not a loser. Not anymore.

He glanced at Georgie, twisting the hem of her skirt. The skirt that, even in a parallel universe, didn't match her cardigan. He released an irritated breath. He could knock out a thousand burpees easily, but working with this train wreck might be his greatest challenge.

Bobby pushed up his glasses, then tapped his iPad. "In thirty seconds, you'll receive a text message with instructions regarding the first challenge. Sometimes, the four of you will be together. Sometimes, you'll be on your own. You're expected to write a blog post about the challenge no more than twenty-four hours after it's been completed."

"And don't forget to always have your phones with you. We'll send each challenge event to you via text message," Hector added, sharing another glance with Bobby.

Jordan watched the CityBeat founders closely. Yes, this was a competition, but it seemed like Bobby and Hector had something else going on beyond just crowning a winner. But he didn't have time to give the eccentric tech giants' motives another thought when a chorus of cell phone pings rang out, and the Dannies sprang up and raced to the door.

He stared at Georgie, who hadn't moved a muscle.

"We've got a meeting with our engineers now, but feel free to stay as long as you like," Bobby said as he joined Hector and left the giant playroom of an office.

The frosted doors closed, and he turned to his partner. "This is it. The competition just started, Georgie."

"I know," she answered, folding her hands in her lap and closing her eyes.

Sweet baby Jesus!

"What are you doing?"

"Processing," she answered.

He exhaled a tight breath, taking out his phone and checking his texts. "Can you process and walk at the same time? I'd settle for a meandering walk at this point."

She opened her eyes. They looked glassy, but she blinked the emotion away. "Do you realize how awful this is for me?"

"For you? What about me?" he balked.

Georgie stood and started for the door, and he was right on her heels. They entered the elevator, and he hit the button for the lobby.

"I should have known," she muttered.

"Known what?"

She threw up her hands. "That it couldn't be that easy. That they'd throw in a curveball."

He should have figured that as well, but he wasn't about to admit that to her.

"It is what it is," he said.

She shook her head and met his gaze in the elevator's reflection. "Where's the challenge event?"

"They just texted an address," he answered.

She frowned. "That's it? Only an address?"

They stared at each other, and he knew she was thinking the same damn thing he was.

How the hell am I going to win with this joker?

He blew out a breath. "We're supposed to use techniques from our respective philosophies to illustrate how to meet a soul mate at this location."

"Okay," she answered, her bottom lip trembling when the doors to the elevator opened, and she took off like a shot.

Christ! She could move in those stupid sandals.

"Hey, we need to talk!" he called after her.

She sprinted the short distance to a car that looked as if it had seen better days and got in. The upside? There was a good chance that even if she drove off, he could run alongside it and keep up.

He gestured for her to roll down the window. She cranked the handle, and the gears screeched and squeaked until the damn thing was cockeyed and half-open.

"I'll meet you there," she huffed, not giving him a second glance as she tried to start the car with no luck.

He took a step back. "It's probably your battery."

She banged her forehead on the steering wheel and emitted the girliest, angry yelp he'd ever heard.

"I know it's the battery! My dad was a mechanic. I was just hoping I could get another month or so out of it."

"My dad was a mechanic, too," he blurted, surprised he'd

admitted it. He'd done his best to keep as much of his old life out of his Marks Perfect Ten Mindset world.

She banged her head on the wheel two more times, and he cringed.

"Could you knock that off. It would be nice to have a teammate without brain damage."

She glanced up at him and scoffed. "Are you ever not a giant douchebag?"

"I prefer His Majesty, the High Emperor of Asshattery."

She shook her head. "I'll call Triple-A, and then I'll meet you at the location."

"No," he answered. He wasn't about to twiddle his thumbs and wait for her car to get a jump, or worse, it may need to be towed. That could take hours.

Georgie's brows knit together. "No?"

"We need to go, Georgie. We have twenty-four hours before the post is due."

She didn't get it.

"I don't know if you know who the Dannies are, but they're not waiting twenty-four hours, and neither am I," he said and opened her car door.

Without thinking, he extended his hand. "The Emperor of Asshattery would like to offer you a ride."

She frowned. "Is this you trying to be charming?"

No, this was him acting like a super nerd, which he was not in any way, shape, or form.

He pointed to his outstretched hand. "Take it or leave it, messy bun girl?"

"Whatever," she murmured and took his hand then stilled, her eyes growing wide.

She felt it, too. When they'd shaken hands in the CityBeat elevator, and all he'd wanted to do was lace his fingers with hers, and he wasn't a hand holder. That kind of bullshit was relegated to the pussy-whipped. In the Marks Perfect Ten Mindset, he advocated touch but only when fucking a perfect ten. Hair pulling, wrist grabbing, and ass biting were all fine and good in the bedroom. But a Marks Perfect Ten man kept his cool in public.

He helped her out of the car but not before brushing his thumb across her knuckles. She had long, slender fingers that fit perfectly in his hand, and the urge to kiss her palm, to bring her lovely fingers to his lips and kiss the tip of each one, a cheesy as hell move if ever there was one, tore through him.

Christ, Marks! Remember the mindset!

"I need to grab my bag," she said, her gaze locked on their joined hands.

"Right," he answered, and, with a reluctance that didn't fit into his Marks Perfect Ten Mindset, he let go.

"Where are you parked?" she asked over her shoulder.

He reached into his pocket, took out his key fob, and unlocked the doors to the BMW SUV parked directly in front of her car. Georgie locked her car door manually, then chuckled and shook her head.

He frowned. "What?"

She made an exaggerated gesture like a model on a game show toward the sleek silver car. "Is this a Marks Perfect Ten Mindset vehicle?" she purred, really overdoing it.

He glanced at the shiny hood and buffed wheels. "Yeah," he answered, coming around to open her door.

"Only luxury cars for the Marks man?" she asked, settling herself inside. Despite that awful cardigan and sandals made for a nativity reenactment, she looked damn good in his car even with that God-awful bun.

He closed her door, came around to his side, and got in. "No, just about any type of car can be a Marks Perfect Ten Mindset car. I suggest that, whatever type of vehicle you have, you keep the interior pristine and the outside washed and waxed."

"Hmm," she replied. "And yes, I have heard of the Dannies. A couple of Danielle's posts popped up in my newsfeed. I wanted to vomit after I read them."

"Do you remember which ones?"

The DannyLyfe blog was his main competition, and he'd made a habit of checking their posts.

She sat back in her seat, jaw set, her cheeks growing pink. "A delightful article titled, How to Please Your Man When You're Under the Weather, which basically said even if you're on death's door, if your guy's in the mood to screw, suck it up, buttercup. Oh, and then there was another about how women should hide their intelligence, so they don't intimidate a potential suitor and another doozy about there being a proper way to kiss."

He pulled out into traffic. "I agree with you. The first two are total bullshit, but there is a right and a wrong way to kiss."

She turned to him in her seat with a furrowed brow and that sweet blush still coloring her cheeks. "No, there is not a *right way* to kiss. A kiss shared between two people who have connected on a deep, substantive level, not lured by looks or status, will always produce the perfect kiss."

He barked out a laugh. "Nope, I can tell you from vast experience, a kiss can be good or bad, completely separate to the level of connection."

"Is that what you preach with all your vast experience to your Marks Perfect Ten Mindset minions?" she asked, using air quotes when she spoke the name of his philosophy.

"I'll remind you that sixty-nine percent of my minions are your minions."

"Don't remind me," she hissed and pressed her fingertips to her eyelids.

They drove in silence as the navigation app led them through Denver.

You have arrived.

He pulled into a parking spot and cut the engine as they unbuckled their seatbelts.

He turned toward her. "We need to get something straight here, Georgie. I help a lot of people improve their lives with my blog posts and recommendations."

She dropped her hands to her lap and leaned in. "Well, so do I, and it has nothing to do with constructing a fake facade."

"You think I'm a fake?" he shot back.

"I think you're all too concerned with appearances and dead wrong that there's a right way to kiss."

"That *superficial stuff* you rail about is called chemistry, and there is scientific data that not only is it real, it's a cornerstone of a healthy relationship. Plus, my blog is all about gaining confidence. And yes, confidence matters when you're kissing."

She slapped her knee and laughed. "Confidence? What about mutual respect and the desire to know someone's heart? And, I bet you're a terrible kisser. You're probably all lips and teeth and tongue."

She opened her mouth and raised her hands, mimicking what looked like a tiger ripping a gazelle to shreds.

Heat rose to his cheeks, and he cupped her face in his hands. "Looks like there's only one way to find out."

Her National Geographic tiger versus gazelle expression vanished, and she held his gaze.

"What do you say?" he asked, baiting her.

"What are you waiting for?" she threw back, not giving a damn inch.

"I'm going to kiss you, Georgie, and it's going to be the best kiss you've ever had."

"Doubtful," she answered in a tight breath.

He tilted her head, and her warm breath tickled his lips. "There's something you need to know about me."

"What's that?" she asked as her hands gripped his forearms.

"I don't settle for anything less than the best. I work damn hard. I finish everything I start, and I always win."

She bit her lip. "That's too bad."

"Oh yeah?" he breathed.

"Yeah. Prepare yourself to lose this competition and this kiss challenge because I'll tell you right now, I have more determination in my little finger than you do in your entire perfect, muscle-bound body."

He brushed his thumb across her petal-soft lips. His pulse raced, and his blood supply headed south, straight to his cock. Georgie closed her eyes and gasped as he made another pass. The tip of her tongue met the pad of his thumb, and a switch flipped inside of him. With her sweet lips still slightly open, he closed the distance between them.

And it was...poetry. Fucking poetry.

She sighed into his mouth, the sweetest sound he'd ever heard, and he slid a hand into her hair, deepening the kiss. He forgot who he was and what he was supposed to be doing. All that existed was this woman and her exquisite mouth. Their tongues met and retreated, licking and caressing. She tasted like that dollop of French vanilla ice cream on warm apple pie. He inhaled, drowning in thoughts of her blue-green eyes and the elegant curve of her neck, meeting the clean line of her jaw.

"Jordan," she whispered between kisses, and his skyrocketing pulse kicked up another notch.

This was the first time she'd uttered his name. Many women had, but none had sounded like this, like music, like a symphony packed into two syllables.

The kiss intensified, their breaths mingling in heated pants. He trailed his fingertips along her neck, past her slight shoulders, and down her back to her slim waist, totally hidden by the damn cardigan. She released his forearms, shrugged out of the bulky garment, and threaded her fingers into the hair at the nape of his neck. She twisted a lock, and the sensation traveled straight to his hard length. He tightened his grip on her hips and slid her body over the console, in what may not have been a Marks Perfect Ten Mindset suave maneuver as a clunk accompanied her surprised yelp.

"My Birkenstock—" she began as her sandal fell off. But he silenced her with a kiss.

Their bodies flush, she straddled him in the tight space. He gripped her ass, which was pretty fucking perfect, and squeezed the firm globes. She arched into him, and he took the opportunity to drop a line of kisses across her jaw to her earlobe.

He rocked her hips, and the friction between them grew hotter. Her skirt inched up, revealing long, toned legs.

Jesus! Maybe there was something to meandering walks. She bucked against him as he dipped a finger inside her panties and found her wet.

So very wet.

Moving together, hands exploring, his cock strained against his pants, he took her earlobe between his teeth. "Georgie, you're—"

BEEP! BEEP! BEEEEEP!

5

Georgie shrieked and shot forward. The horn silenced, and she stared into Jordan's eyes, her trifecta frozen, their imaginary mouths hanging open. Their literary minds momentarily scrambled, just like hers.

Holy Marks Perfect Ten Mindset kiss!

She cleared her throat. "I can certainly tell that you've put a lot of thought into your...technique," she said, trying to establish some semblance of professionalism, but her tingling lips and straddling thighs seriously put a kink in that.

He nodded. "It's definitely something I've thought a great deal about. You know, lips and stuff."

"And hands," she offered.

Another nod from the Emperor of Asshattery. "Yes, hands are a crucial element in the Marks Perfect Ten Mindset kissing protocol."

"Oh, so it's a protocol?" she asked as if they were discussing the weather.

Crap city! Was she making small talk now, on Jordan's lap?

"Yes, like I'm sure the Own the Eights method employs," he replied.

"Yes, all the protocols when it comes to kissing. I mean, all the un-superficial protocols."

Was un-superficial a word? The trifecta shook their heads. Gah!

"Sure, that sounds entirely in line with your blog's vibe," he offered.

A slice of silence stretched between them as they watched each other the way one would observe an alien species.

"You should probably let go of my butt," she said with a little grin, then wiped the expression off her face. Who the hell smiles when they ask someone to release their ass?

His hands shot up into the air as if he were under arrest. "Jesus! Of course!"

Without the support of his big, strong hands holding her up, because God help her, they were big, and they were strong, she fell back and hit the steering wheel, bumping the horn and sending another chorus of beeps into the...

Parking lot?

"Where are we?" she asked, craning her head. There wasn't a lot of maneuverability straddling a large man in the front seat of a luxury SUV.

"We're at an organic market."

She nodded. "That makes sense for me. I blog about the importance of mindful eating and how that is an essential attribute of an eight."

"Me too. Diet is a key component of the Marks Perfect Ten Mindset."

Her jaw dropped. There was no way his blog shared this ideology with hers.

"Right." She scoffed. "You've gotta be all ripped and ready to tear off your shirt at a moment's notice. My blog takes a more holistic approach. A responsibly sourced food supply and organic farming practices mean something to my followers.

Meeting an eight at the market isn't about rocking killer forearms. It's about employing an outlook that considers the planet when searching for your soul mate."

He frowned. "Are you talking about the killer forearms you're still gripping with some gusto, I may add."

She dropped her hands. Stupid alluring forearms! She may be straddling his lap, but she put on her game face. This was a competition, after all, and Jordan Marks, with his shallow mindset, was her competitor.

Jane, Lizzie, and Hermione cheered!

She shifted her hips and brushed against his very large, rock-hard—

STOP! Her trifecta squirted her with an imaginary water cannon.

She plastered on a smirk. "What a setback for the Marks Perfect Ten Mindset, getting all hot and bothered over an *eight*."

He schooled his perfect features. "I am not hot and bothered, and I didn't hear you complaining during that…"

"Technique demonstration," she supplied. Despite her lips screaming to be reattached to his, that couldn't happen again.

No way!

"Right, a technique demonstration that your little sighs and lusty moans seemed to indicate you thoroughly enjoyed," he answered, meeting her smirk with one of his own.

She gasped. "Lusty moans?"

He gave her a cocky shrug. "You did say my name on a pretty sexy sigh."

Double crap! It had slipped out. But that kiss was so—

Another water cannon blast from the trifecta knocked her back on track.

"So, you think I'm sexy?" she countered.

A muscle ticked in his jaw. "What I think is that the demonstration is over. You need to slip back into that Own the Eights cardigan, and we need to complete the first challenge."

"Exactly what I was thinking," she replied, twisting off his lap and falling over the console into the passenger seat.

"And don't forget your Julius Caesar sandals," he said, but when she glanced up from collecting her shoes, he looked dazed and almost as off-kilter as she felt.

She pulled on her cardigan, got out of the Beamer, and joined him outside the market. She peeked inside. The aisles buzzed with young professionals. A little after seven o'clock, the after-work crowd perused the organic fare, many congregating near the prepared food counter and the salad bar.

"Do you think the Dannies are here?" she asked.

They passed through the sliding glass doors, and he glanced around. "You go left, and I'll go right. Let's do a sweep and check. I'll meet you at the baby carrots."

"Okay," she answered, not at all keen on taking direction from this guy. But, like it or not, they had to work together.

She strolled the length of the produce section with no Dannies in sight, when a guy in ripped jeans and a Save the Whales shirt bumped into her.

"So sorry," he said with a polite nod. "I'm looking for the cucumbers."

She gestured over her shoulder. "Over there, by the zucchini."

"Thanks," he said and went on with his shopping.

"Are you getting a head start? You were supposed to be scoping out the joint for the Dannies."

Jordan Marks narrowed his eyes, and she groaned.

"There are no Dannies on my side of the store. What about you? Did you see them?"

He shook his head. "I did a complete sweep. They're not

here. Hector and Bobby must have sent them to another store or maybe a separate challenge."

She crossed her arms. "Well, we're here. Let's see this Perfect Ten Mindset in action."

"You want to watch?" he asked with a raised eyebrow.

"Yeah, I need to know how much damage control will have to be done after you're arrested for harassing women in a grocery store."

"I don't need to stalk women, Georgie," he said, all stupid sexy forearms and smug smirk.

"Sure," she said, casting a skeptical look.

He glanced around the bustling market. "You'll see. It's like bees to honey."

"Then buzz off and get to work," she countered.

The hint of a smile pulled at his lips, and his dimple appeared.

His Brice Casey dimple.

"Hang back. I can't have your eight-vibe encroaching on my *ten-ness*."

"*Ten-ness*?" she fired off.

"Fine, my awesomeness. Do you like that better?"

She flapped her hands and buzzed, doing her best bee impression.

"Jesus, Georgie," he balked then started down an aisle.

She grabbed a basket and tossed in a tube of vegan cookie dough as she *hung back* and observed the Emperor of Asshattery.

And she wasn't the only one watching.

Every woman he passed turned and stared. They straightened up, their cheeks growing pink. A petite redhead threw him a furtive glance then reached for a jar of honey on a high shelf.

Stupid honey!

"Oh, sir, could you give me a hand?" she asked through her lashes.

Gag!

"Would you like me to lift you up, or should I just get it for you myself," he purred.

Double gag!

"I'd jump, but these shoes make it so hard," she cooed, then kicked up her foot to reveal a lot of leg and a fire engine red stiletto.

Jordan easily procured the jar and handed it to her. "I don't want anything to ruin those heels, and we should probably exchange numbers in case you need some help with that honey. You know, later on, if the lid's stuck and you can't get it open." He leaned in. "Honey can get sticky."

"So sticky," the woman repeated, completely under his spell, then snapped out of it, grabbed her phone, and thrust it into Jordan's hand.

Sheesh! So much for playing hard to get!

While they entered their digits, he stole a glance over his shoulder and winked at her.

He was such the Emperor of Asshattery!

She mouthed the word *boring* then mimicked falling asleep.

And what did this lady even know about Jordan, besides the fact that he was good-looking and competent enough to retrieve a jar of honey? For Pete's sake! Mr. Tuesday could do that, probably, maybe? Oh, who was she kidding? She was lucky if her sweet pup only ruined one pair of shoes a week instead of two. But it didn't matter.

"You'll find me in your contacts under Layla," the redhead said, handing Jordan back his phone.

"I'll be under Jordan," he replied smoothly as a wave of nausea washed over her.

The redhead swished her perfect tumbled curls and headed up the aisle.

Jordan crossed his arms and leaned against the shelf. "What did I say? Bees to honey. Now, what was that, ten seconds to get her number?" He scratched his chin with a theatrical flair. "Nah, probably eight seconds. It looks like I'm the one owning the eights tonight, Georgie Jensen."

"Jackass," she muttered under her breath, throwing a few more items into her basket.

"Your turn, Messy Bun."

Messy Bun! Of all the nicknames!

She pushed up onto her tiptoes in a sad attempt to be eye level with the man who just ruined honey for her. "Try to understand this. The person who's going to like me, Jordan-totally-not-owning-the-eights, is going to be able to see past my bun. He'll see me for the person I am on the inside. And, in fact, he'll love this bun. He won't be able to get enough of it."

Jordan glanced at his watch. "That's exactly what I'd expect someone in a cardigan to say. Now stop stalling."

How could she have engaged in a lip-lock with this Slick Rick Perfect Ten cretin? She set off, searching the store for her Save the Whales guy.

"Cucumbers!" she whispered, remembering their brief conversation.

She hurried back to the produce section and found her guy still perusing the vegetables.

"Need any help handling that cucumber?" she asked, the words escaping her mouth a microsecond before she realized how perverted that question sounded.

Jordan coughed. "So smooth."

She glared at him as he pretended to search for a head of lettuce.

"Excuse me?" Save the Whales asked, his gaze bouncing between herself and Jordan.

She pulled out her beauty queen smile—desperate times called for desperate measures. "I wanted to make sure you found the cucumbers."

He held up the vegetable, and she leaned in to study it.

"You don't want that one. You want a bigger one."

"Holy shit!" Jordan fake coughed.

She lifted her chin and tried to ignore the six-foot-four man, now laugh-hacking all over the cilantro. "That cucumber's too small. Now, if you choose one that's too big, it may not taste as good and be a bit too seedy. What you want is a nice medium-sized one. You'll also want to check it for flexibility."

"What?" the guy asked, a little dazed.

She reached out, and Save the Whales gave her the vegetable.

She felt the cucumber carefully, slowly wrapping her hands around the cylindrical food. "See what I'm doing, and see how the cucumber is bending?"

Save the Whale's eyes had gone wide as she massaged the vegetable, bending it side to side to show its flexibility.

"Jesus Christ on a cracker," Jordan barked out in an exaggerated cough like a man dying of the Spanish flu.

Save the Whales glanced over at him. "Do you think that guy's all right?"

"He's fine." She turned to Jordan. "Sir, you should check out the herbal teas on aisle five. They're great for cough suppression."

Red-faced, Jordan blinked back tears of laughter and moved down the row toward a rack of bananas.

"You really want to make sure you've got a firm cucumber," she continued, because, despite the whole phallic symbolism of this convo, once the cucumber door opens, there's no going back.

"My cucumber's not firm?" Save the Whales asked as the hacking laughter of Jordan Marks again tore through the produce department.

"No, you need it to be a little firmer."

Save the Whales stared at the vegetable. "Thanks for the tip."

"And speaking of tips..." she continued.

A round of thuds erupted behind her. Jordan, in a hissy fit of laughter, had bumped into a display of onions.

She ignored him and pressed on. "You'll want to make sure it's firm all the way to the ends or tips."

Save the Whales stared at the bin of cucumbers. "All this time I've been eating cucumbers, I never knew to check for firmness."

"They're also actually a fruit because they come from a flower and contain seeds, but I've probably gone way overboard with the cucumber lecture," she said with an embarrassed smile.

Save the Whales chose a new, firm cucumber, added it to his basket, then shifted from foot to foot. "Do you live around here?"

Georgie's trifecta perked up.

"Not too far from here," she answered *as cool as a cucumber* and snuck a glance at Jordan.

"I'm new to the city. Could I get your number, and maybe we could hang out and make cucumber salad?"

Triumph surged through her veins. If this were a superhero movie, she'd levitate a few feet above the ground, blast Jordan with her laser beam eyes, and give the nice whale activist her number. Unfortunately, she'd never come into contact with a radioactive spider, nor did she hail from a distant superpower planet, so she'd have to settle for the latter.

But it was still a win for her Own the Eights philosophy.

She expected to hear another bout of cough-laughter, but when she glanced over her shoulder, this time, she'd found Jordan stock still, clutching a potato with a vengeance completely undeserving of the root vegetable. She threw him a sweet screw-you smile and exchanged numbers with...

"Steve," she said, glancing at her phone's screen where he'd entered his information.

"Georgie," he said, staring at his. "Is that short for Georgia?"

"No, Georgiana."

Steve smiled. "That's a lovely name for a lovely—"

The cough was gone, but the guttural sound of Jordan clearing his throat echoed off the organic beets and stopped Steve from finishing his sentence.

She took a step back and smiled at her Save the Whales conquest. "I should finish my shopping. But I hope I'll see you around, Steve."

"Yeah, me too. Nice to meet you, Georgie," Steve replied with a kind smile, apropos of one who cares deeply for the ocean, then weaved his way toward the checkout.

She blew out a relieved breath when she felt Jordan come up behind her, and she had the bizarre desire to lean back into his brick wall of a torso. Gah! Why did that have to be her first thought? She'd done it! She'd proved her method was just as good as his, but she couldn't remember one thing about Save the Whales Steve other than his shirt.

With Jordan, she remembered everything. His clean scent. How his green eyes darkened when he gazed at her. The four freckles on his left forearm that looked like the handle of the big dipper. She tensed as her lady parts begged to climb back onto his lap and rock her body against his hard—"

"Cucumber," Jordan said, and she gasped, shaking all thoughts of doing anything with his cucumber out of her head.

This lapse in judgment was just the superficial cavewoman

who dwelled in the primitive brainstem of every woman, trying to claw her way past the rational Own the Eights intelligent, conscientious side of her and procreate with this, or any other, member of the male species. But she was an eights gal and that meant that Jordan and his Perfect Ten Mindset was nothing she wanted in her life.

She picked up a cucumber and threw it into her basket. "I think a cucumber salad with dinner sounds delightful." She snagged another. "Here, you look like you could use a cucumber, too."

He waved off the vegetable. "I think you've ruined cucumbers for me."

"Suit yourself. I'm going to go pay for my groceries," she said, dropping the second cucumber into her basket. She turned to go but froze when he spoke.

"Why did you pick him?"

She studied his expression. "Steve?"

"Yeah, Save the Whales Hipster Steve. Why did you think he was an eight?"

Was Jordan jealous?

She held his gaze. "By partaking in certain activities, you prove your *eight-ness*."

"*Eight-ness*?" he repeated skeptically.

"You said *ten-ness*. So, by default, I get *eight-ness*."

He ran a hand through his perfect hair. "Was it the whale shirt?"

She weighed the question. "There are subtle eights signs that show that a person cares about bigger things than just themselves. You can find these attributes in how someone dresses, in what they buy, and how they act. His shirt tells me there's a good chance he volunteers to help animals and probably cares deeply about the environment."

"Why couldn't a ten do all those things, too?" Jordan shot back.

She cocked her head to the side. "When was the last time you volunteered at an animal shelter or participated in a community cleanup?"

He shook his head and stared past her shoulder.

"Aha! See, that's what makes Steve an eight and you, just a ten."

"Just because I'm not wearing a Greenpeace shirt doesn't mean I don't care about the planet or work my ass off."

"But you do it for yourself."

"I help a lot of people become—"

"Superficial wankers," she cut in.

He frowned. "No, healthier and happier. I give people a road map to their best life. I show them their greatness, their perfection."

She took a step toward him. "Perfection is just an illusion."

He leaned in, his lips inches from hers. "Only to those too scared or too jaded to reach for it."

What was it about this asshat? One minute, she couldn't care less if he fell off the face of the earth. The next, every cell in her body ached for his touch. And where was her trifecta? They couldn't be falling for Jordan's artificial antics.

"I'll meet you outside," she said in a shaky breath and headed for the self-checkout.

Mindlessly, she scanned and bagged her items. Her blood sugar had to be low. That had to be it. Her trifecta nodded, all of them a little off balance. Between the meeting at CityBeat, that kiss in Jordan's car, and the tense scene next to the cucumbers, she must be damn near ready to pass out.

She grabbed her groceries, left the market, and pulled out the tube of vegan chocolate chip cookie dough. Without thinking, she ripped the top of the tube open with her teeth and squeezed the chocolaty goodness into her mouth.

"What the hell are you eating?"

She turned to see Jordan standing by a bench.

"Cookie dough," she tried to say with a mouthful of gooey deliciousness.

His eyes went wide as if she'd morphed into a two-headed monster.

She swallowed. "It's vegan! Relax!"

Mortification marred his symmetrically perfect face. "I don't care if it's vegan. It's still a tube of cookie dough."

She squeezed the cylinder and took another mouthful. "It's delicious, and the company donates a portion of its profits to the rainforest."

"Are you trying to say that this disgusting display of complete lack of willpower is actually a civic good deed?" he sneered.

"Yes," she answered, then hummed her delight and swallowed the raw vegan dough.

Jordan shook his head, sat down, then took out his phone.

"What are you doing? Are you texting your honey girl already?" she asked, plopping down next to him.

"No, I'm deleting *Layla*. She has a name, Georgie. She's a person."

Georgie tried to scoff, but it was damn hard to appear incredulous with a mouthful of delicious vegan cookie dough. Still, she was not going to be lectured about respecting women from the likes of the Marks Perfect Ten Mindset guru.

She dropped the tube of dough into her recyclable bag. "Why? Layla's not hot enough for you? Not the perfect ten woman you've been dreaming of finding?"

He pinned her with his gaze. "My focus is on this competition, Georgiana."

The breath caught in her throat. He'd called her by her full name, and the four syllables had never sounded so sensual. Jane Eyre passed fans to Lizzie and Hermione, and she could have used one, too.

"What if *Layla* calls you?" she asked, going for nonchalance.

His eyes flicked back to the phone. "She'll get the number to make a donation to the local public library."

Georgie gasped. "You wrong-numbered her?"

Her pulse shot up. Her mouth grew dry. Maybe it was all the organic sugar and responsibly sourced chocolate, but she felt exactly like she had when he'd run by the bookshop earlier in the day. She steadied herself. Why should she care if he gave some chick the wrong number? He meant nothing to her.

"We should exchange contact information," he said, followed by a resigned sigh.

"You want my number? My real number?"

"And address. Like it or not, if we want to beat the Dannies, we need to work together."

Her trifecta shrugged. The man did have a point.

They traded phones, and she bit back a grin, entering her information.

"Why are you smiling?" he asked, eyes glued to her phone screen.

She glanced at him. "How can you tell I'm smiling? You're not even looking at me."

"I just can, and don't break my phone."

"I won't break your phone. Here, you'll find me under Messy Bun."

The corner of his mouth curled up, and he handed her back her smartphone.

"What did you do?" she asked, then glanced down to see the new contact of the Emperor of Asshattery. She bit back a grin. "I'm glad you've come to terms with who you really are."

"Oh, I know who I am. I'm just not sure if you're bright enough to remember my real name, so I went with the moniker that would be the easiest for you to recall."

And...the emperor was back.

She came to her feet. "Okay, well, goodbye."

He shot up. "Goodbye?"

"Yeah, we did the whole grocery store challenge and now—"

"Now, we strategize. We come up with a plan," he answered, cutting her off.

"Well, I need to get back to my car and call for a jump. Then, I need to go home and feed my dog."

"Sergeant Wednesday?" he asked, but his smirk said he knew damn well that wasn't her sweet pup's name.

"Mr. Tuesday," she corrected.

"All right, then. Let's go."

"Go where?"

"To get your car, Georgiana. I'll drive you back and give you a jump."

There he was with the *Georgiana* again.

She ignored the butterflies in her belly. "That's okay. I can walk."

He glanced around. "It's dark out."

She shook her head. "It's dusk."

"It's more dark than light," he replied, exasperation infused in his tone.

"Yeah, that's the definition of dusk," she threw back.

He took a step toward her. "Can we not argue about this? I'm not letting you walk through the city all alone at night."

She lifted her chin. "At dusk."

"Jesus! At dusk! I'm not leaving you alone at dusk," he answered in full-blown frustration mode.

She was about to recommend that he try a guided meditation to chill out when warmth radiated through her hand. She glanced down and found that somewhere in their tussle over the definition of dusk, he'd taken her hand into his.

His expression softened. "Let me drive you back to your car and give it a jump. Then we can head to your place and walk Officer Friday."

"It's Mr. Tuesday," she corrected, but this time, without the sass.

He looked at their hands then let go, taking a step back. "Sorry, I didn't mean to..."

Despite despising ninety-nine percent about this guy, she liked the way her hand felt in his. The warmth. The protective sweetness. The heat that said these hands want to grip your ass and kiss you like there's no tomorrow.

But that could not happen. Not again.

"No more technique demonstrations. We have to act like professionals," she said, the words tasting bitter and disingenuous.

He flexed his hands, then crossed his arms. "I agree. From here on out, it's all about the blog competition," he supplied, but his declaration didn't quiet the butterflies still flapping away in her belly.

You cannot fall for this ten, Georgie.

Her trifecta was back, minus the fans, and armed with girl power.

Think of Brice Casey. Think of your dreams.

She pushed away all thoughts of Jordan's lips, and his hands, and his expression after Save the Whales Steve asked for her number.

They may have to work together, but one thing was crystal clear, he was still her competition.

Back in the game, she ignored those pesky butterflies. "Deal. We're all business from here on out. Let's go."

6

Jordan stared at the brake lights of the car in front of him and flipped on his blinker the second after the lead car's right turn signal illuminated.

He wasn't just following any car. He was behind Georgie's car and following her to her place, which just happened to be a block away from his rental.

He glanced over at the passenger seat then inhaled. Her scent still lingered in his SUV. Probably some hippie vanilla lotion or Own the Eights earth-friendly shampoo. It was...nice. He shook his head and cranked up the air-conditioning.

This messy bun girl could not get into his head. Not only was she his competition, but she also did not fit the definition of a Marks Perfect Ten Mindset partner, or did she?

Hell no! Of course, she didn't. Those damned shoes were an immediate disqualifier. Throw in the cardigan and the glasses on a chain, and she might as well be one of the before pictures his clients loved to post once they'd attained the Marks Perfect Ten Mindset body and lifestyle.

He pressed his lips into a tight line. Dammit! She was there, too.

And that kiss! Had Georgie not bumped the horn, who knows what would have happened.

What had gotten into him? Granted, it had been a while since he'd slept with a woman. For all the dating and lifestyle posts he'd written, in reality, he'd done very little of it himself these past few years. Sure, he'd blogged about the best places to meet a Marks Perfect Ten Mindset soul mate, but that didn't mean it left him any time to find his Marks Perfect Ten match.

And Georgie was infuriating. Nobody pressed his buttons. Nobody teased him—anymore.

That had to be it! She riled him up. That, and the stress of the competition, had momentarily blinded him from his goals.

But she did have one hell of an ass hidden beneath that hideous skirt.

Dammit! Knock it off, Marks!

He squeezed the steering wheel as her voice cut through his thoughts.

Jordan.

It made him hard just thinking about it.

Georgie Jensen got him hard...again.

Georgie's car slowed and came to a stop in front of a craftsman style bungalow, and he cut the ignition on his BMW and glanced down at his lap. "She is not for us," he scolded, then glanced up to find Georgie standing right outside, watching him.

Shit!

"Everything all right in there?" she asked as he got out.

"Yes," he answered, not at all excited that they were parked directly beneath a lamppost, emitting what seemed like way too much light. He could use a little darkness to hide what he was sure was a decent bulge in his pants.

"I only ask because it looked like you were talking to your—"

"I was stretching my neck," he replied tersely.

"Your neck?" she repeated as if it were a foreign concept.

It was time to get it together.

"Yes, if you're not familiar with anatomy, the neck is the part that connects the head to the body."

She parted her lips, undoubtedly ready to throw an insult his way when the door to a truck parked across the street opened, and a woman exited the vehicle.

"Hey, Jordan!" she called as Georgie's playful smirk vanished.

"Did you invite a date to my house? I saw you texting right after you jump-started my car. I should have known," she snapped, incredulity permeating her words.

He bit back a grin. "That's just Ginger."

"Oh, good, it's *just* Ginger," she whisper-shouted.

"I know her from my gym. And just for the record, I noticed that you were on your phone while I was bringing your car back to life," he answered.

Now it was his turn to sport a shit-eating grin. Because thanks to all that worry about sporting a hard-on, he'd forgotten that he'd sent the text right after he'd set an alert to go off any time the Dannies posted.

"You really put the ass in asshattery," she hissed, crossing her arms.

"It's good to see you, Jordan," came a man's voice.

Georgie whipped her head around and stared into the street as a burly man covered in tattoos, carrying a toolbox and a car battery, joined Ginger on the sidewalk.

"Jordan, who are these people?" Georgie asked, moving closer to him.

The man gestured with his chin. "Is this the two thousand VW Rabbit that needs the new battery?"

"Yeah, it sure is, Zeke. Thanks for doing me this favor." He glanced at Georgie and then to his friends. "Georgie Jensen, meet Ginger and Zeke Jones."

"Nice to meet you, Georgie. We'll be done in no time flat,"

Ginger said, shaking Georgie's hand as Zeke gave her a friendly nod.

"Do you mind unlocking the car and popping the hood, miss?" Zeke asked, setting up a portable light.

Georgie's gaze bounced between the people attending to her car. "What's going on?"

"Zeke and Ginger are clients of mine at the gym. They own a garage nearby. I texted them to see if they could get you a new battery."

"Hand me your keys, hun," Ginger said with an easy grin.

With a glazed look, Georgie complied, then turned to him, eyes wide. "Why did you do this, Jordan?"

Shit! Why did he do this? The minute he got her car running, the thought of her stranded somewhere drove him to bust out his phone and text Zeke and Ginger her address, asking them to switch out her battery. But he couldn't admit that.

He cleared his throat. "If I'm going to be forced to work with you, you're going to need a reliable car. I can't have you stuck on the side of the road screwing up my chance at winning the contest."

Even with the patchy lamplight, he could see the warmth in her blue-green eyes dissipate.

She clucked her tongue. "For a second, I thought there might actually be a human being inhabiting your body. Turns out, I was wrong."

"Yeah, the Marks Perfect Ten Mindset people are superhumans, so it makes sense you'd make that mistake," he rallied back.

"More like super douchebags," she murmured when the grumble of an engine purring to life caught their attention.

"My car started! How did you do that so quickly?" Georgie asked.

Zeke wiped his hands on a rag. "Changing a battery isn't very hard, but you should come in and see us if your car needs anything else. A friend of Jordan's is a friend of ours."

"He's not my..." Georgie began, but she stopped herself and softened her expression. "Thank you so much for changing the battery. What do I owe you?"

Ginger waved her off. "Jordan took care of it with a few extra training sessions on the house, so we're good."

"Thanks, guys!" he called as Ginger and Zeke got back into their vehicle.

"I can't believe you did that," Georgie said as the truck disappeared down the road.

He shifted his stance. "Like I said, I can't have you ruining my chances."

She groaned and stared up at the night sky. "This is a barrel of laughs, hanging out with you, but I should really get to my dog."

"Lead the way," he said and followed her up the brick path to her front door.

She glanced at him over her shoulder. "It may be a little messy inside. I wasn't expecting to bring anyone home with me. But...it's not that I'm *not* able to meet an eight and bring him back to my place to connect on a deeper level," she added, shifting her grocery bag from hand to hand.

"Right," he replied, not sure what the hell to say to that.

She turned and pressed her back to the door. "And it's not like we'd jump right into bed, this eight that I hypothetically met and invited back to my home. We'd probably play chess or checkers or talk. That's what Owning the Eights is all about, and as the creator of the blog and a woman in charge of her body and her sexuality, that's just what would happen," she finished, looking just as confused by that quasi-rant as he was.

Away from the road and the streetlights, shadows cast on her face as a wisp of hair came free of her bun and blew across her cheek. He raised his hand to brush it back but stopped himself.

She is your competition.

He could hear Deacon's voice in the breeze, laying down the law, training him to be the best.

He dropped his hand to his side. "Georgiana, I don't care what your place looks like. We're here to talk strategy. I'm not Save the Whales Steve looking to connect my soul to yours or whatever bullshit language you use to describe the mating habits of an eight."

"There's the asshat," she said with what he would have sworn was a touch of disappointment as she unlocked the door.

But before he could throw back a barb about her shoes or her mismatched clothing, the excited yelps of Mr. Tuesday, yes, he knew the dog's name, pulled Georgie's attention away from him.

"How is my bestest boy?" she cooed as they entered the house.

"Bestest isn't a real word," he corrected. He knew damned well that she'd pegged him as a superficial jerk, and it was easier to play the part. He needed the distance. When he'd let his guard down, he'd either kissed her, called in a favor to have her car serviced, or held her hand like some goofy tween at the movies.

Georgie slipped a leash off a hook by the door and attached it to the dog's collar. "I'll just be a minute. Make yourself comfortable...but, not too comfortable." She glanced around as if the moment she'd left, she expected him to go all stealth super-spy, copying her laptop's hard drive and planting listening devices in her lamps.

He gave her his best Emperor of Asshattery face. "What do you think I'm going to do? Bust out your yoga mat or take a meandering walk and raid your refrigerator? Don't worry, I won't disrupt your home's feng shui."

"Do you even know what feng shui is?" she asked, halfway out the door, her dog pulling and skittering about at her feet.

He plastered on his signature Jordan Marks smirk. "No, but I'd bet my Beamer that you do."

Georgie released an irritated groan and left the house with her animated dog.

With the place Georgie and dog-free, he inhaled. There was that smell again. Sweet vanilla. She'd probably bought a candle from some company that gave a villager a donkey with each purchase. That's what an eight would do. But he cared about the environment, too. Being a ten did not mean screwing over the planet or anyone or anything for that matter. He took a meandering walk around her living room, and on every shelf, table, and even stacked in the corners, he found books. Lots of books. It made sense. She did own a bookstore. A hardback of Steinbeck's *East of Eden* caught his eye when he saw what could only be described as a shrine with little candles and doll figurines.

The door to the bungalow opened, and an excited Mr. Tuesday burst into the room and made a beeline toward him.

"You found my trifecta," she said, hanging the leash back on the hook.

The dog came to his side, and he scratched between his ears. "I noticed your copy of *East of Eden*."

"You like Steinbeck?" she asked, heading for the kitchen as Mr. Tuesday followed right on her heels.

"Yeah, I double-majored in English and Kinesiology," he answered.

"Yeah, right, and I minored in Underwater Basket Weaving," she called over the sound of a can opener.

She didn't believe him. He was about to set her straight when he caught his reflection in the front window. He may not be the scrawny kid hidden away in a quiet corner of the library anymore, but that didn't mean he'd lost his love of literature.

"*Jane Eyre, Pride and Prejudice,* and *Harry Potter,*" he said, turning to the books prominently featured on the shelf.

She joined him and lovingly ran her finger down the worn spine of Jane Austen's *Pride and Prejudice.* "These are my favorites."

He eyed the books. "Interesting combo. I can appreciate the similarities in *Jane Eyre* and *Pride and Prejudice,* but how does *Harry Potter* fit in?"

She smiled, but it didn't reach her eyes. "I had a weird childhood. Jane from *Jane Eyre,* Lizzie from *Pride and Prejudice,* and Hermione from *Harry Potter* became my girl squad."

"Girl squad?" he repeated with a chuckle.

"You can laugh all you like, Mr. Marks Perfect Ten Mindset. But these books got me through some tough times."

"Comics did that for me when I was a kid," he said softly, then glanced at her and found her watching him closely.

Did he just share that comics were his escape as a kid? Dammit! He looked back at the shelf, then tapped a framed picture of a man standing next to a little girl, holding what looked like a credit card. "Is that you?"

"Yeah, that's my dad and me the day I got my very own library card. My dad was a mechanic, and he really loved books. He was kind of a Renaissance man, a Jack of all trades."

"And your mom?"

Georgie looked away. "She splits her time between Denver and her homes in Aspen and St. Croix."

He took a step back and whistled. "I would not have pegged you as someone who came from money."

"I didn't. My parents divorced when I was young, and my mom married into it," she answered, her gaze trained on the photograph.

"But still, if your mom is wealthy now—"

"That has nothing to do with me, nor do I want a penny of her money. I live my own life, and I make my own rules, Jordan," she answered, heat flashing in her blue-green eyes.

"Sorry, I didn't mean to pry."

"It's fine," she answered with that same smile that didn't quite reach her eyes. "Come into the kitchen. The least I can do is feed you after you had your friends fix my car."

What the hell was he doing? Twenty-four hours ago, Georgie Jensen didn't even exist to him. He'd been living in the twilight zone from the moment she'd barreled into his life, yelling for him to catch her dog.

"Can you chop a cucumber?" she asked, holding out the vegetable.

"Yes, of course, I can. If you read the Marks Perfect Ten blog, you'd learn that cucumbers contain silica, which is essential for maintaining healthy connective tissue," he said, choosing a knife from a block on the counter and joining her at the cutting board.

"If you read the Own the Eights blog, you'd know that what we're eating tonight is a cucumber, tomato, and basil salad, which contains vitamin C," she threw back as she chopped a tomato.

"I already knew that," he mumbled.

"Just dice the cucumber, emperor."

He sliced the vegetable. "You should really have a protein to go with this."

"I do," she answered and gestured with her chin toward two salmon fillets in a glass dish.

Shit. This was a pretty decent meal.

"The fish is from last night. I like to make extra to eat as left-overs the next day."

Double shit. He suggested doing that, too.

Georgie took his perfectly diced cucumber and added it to

the basil and tomatoes with a pinch of salt and a dash of pepper. She pulled two plates from the cabinet, then proceeded to make him a plate.

"Is this okay?" she asked, handing him a fork and napkin.

It was more than okay. He mostly ate alone. Breakfast at home. A protein shake in his office at the gym and dinner either in front of the computer or proofing an article for a blog post.

"Yeah, it's great. Thanks," he said, taking the plate.

Her cheeks grew pink. "We can eat on the couch. My kitchen table is a little full."

He glanced over at the small table, teeming with books and legal pads.

"No problem."

He followed her out of the kitchen and sat down next to her on the couch.

"So, this is your life?"

Christ! He sounded like an idiot!

She chuckled through a bite of salmon. "I'm sure it's not as glamorous as yours. You're probably on the VIP list at every fancy restaurant and take out a different perfect ten woman every night."

If she only knew.

"Something like that," he said and took a bite.

"Should we look at the schedule?" she asked, reaching down and pulling the sheet of paper out of her purse as Mr. Tuesday sauntered to him and curled up around his feet.

Georgie gasped. "Look at that! You can't be completely void of a soul if Mr. Tuesday likes you."

"Only partially void," he said and took another bite of the salmon. The whole meal was fucking delicious, but hell if he was about to cop to loving her leftovers.

She sat cross-legged and set her plate on the coffee table. "Everything is a little cryptic on this, except for the last event. It looks like the competition ends at the Denver Trot, and it's going to be live-streamed onto the CityBeat site." She frowned. "Is that a dance, like a foxtrot?"

Now it was his turn to laugh. He finished the fucking delicious food and set his empty plate next to hers. "It's a 10K race."

She grimaced. "Like running?"

"Yeah, that's generally what's expected in a race."

"How many miles is a 10K?"

"Just six point two."

Her jaw dropped. "Of running? Over six miles of straight running without any scary clowns or grizzly bears chasing you?"

"Let me see that," he said, holding out his hand. She passed him the schedule, and he scanned it quickly. "It says here we'll accumulate our final likes as we complete the race."

Georgie leaned back and rested her head on the couch cushion. "The Dannies will probably perform CPR and save a man's life on the race route. And I'm warning you now, I'm not a runner. I can sprint. I can bust out of a ballroom and be halfway down the block like nobody's business, but I'm not a runner."

"You are now," he shot back.

She sat forward. "No, I promise you, I'm not."

This was not good. There was no damn way he'd be meandering his way through the Denver Trot—especially if it's going to be live-streamed for millions to see.

"Even if I have to throw you over my shoulder, your ass is crossing that finish line, Georgiana. Marks Perfect Ten Rule number one, you always finish what you start."

She narrowed her gaze. "Own the Eights Rule number one is to honor who you are on the inside. If that means not winning a race, then so be it."

"We're not losing that race. I'll train you every day if I have to, but this is non-negotiable."

"Winning isn't everything," she bit out, fire raging in her eyes.

He leaned in. "Yeah, it is."

Mr. Tuesday must have sensed the shift in the atmosphere. He scrambled over to a doggie bed on the other side of the room, but not before bumping into a pile of books stacked on the corner of the coffee table.

Her gaze shifted to the books, and she gasped. "I better get that," she exclaimed and reached over him.

Jesus! What book could have her jumping into his lap to scoop it up? And then he looked.

The Kama Sutra by Vatsyayana: Annotated: English Translation.

"That's the book with all the different sexual positions, isn't it?" he asked, craning his head to get a better look.

She squirmed in his lap, knocking it open to...

Hello, reverse cowgirl.

Her cheeks had gone full crimson. "It's nothing. It's for research."

He plucked the book from her hands and held it just out of her reach. "So, this is what Own the Eights is really about." He flipped a page and glanced at a rather lovely illustration of a couple in the sixty-nine position.

She straddled him, pushing up onto her knees and reached for the book. "It is a lot more than just sex positions. The *Kama Sutra* is a guide to maintaining a healthy love life and finding emotional fulfillment," she huffed, clambering to get the paperback.

He flipped a page and glanced up. "And that would all happen in the doggie-style position, according to this."

"You're so obtuse, Jordan," she snapped, grasping his thigh for balance, then stilled and stared into his eyes.

Fuck!

For a third time today, Georgie Jensen had given him an erection. An erection her hand had just grazed.

"Sexual activity is a good stress reliever," she said, the bite in her tone replaced with a sexy as sin little rasp.

His free hand had somehow made it to her hip, and he pulled her in a fraction closer. "I've read a few studies on that."

Her pupils dilated. "And while the *Kama Sutra* does include an erotic element, the overarching theme is how to live a fulfilling life with a supportive, loving partner."

"There's data that supports that claim, too. You know, science and shit," he added, on the verge of losing himself in her damned enticing eyes.

"Yeah, all the science and shit," she replied in a tight whisper as her shallow breaths tickled his chin.

He swallowed hard. "Competitions are stressful."

"Very stressful," she agreed.

"And finding a release for that stress would make us better competitors," he continued, not at all thinking about the peer-reviewed studies that supported his point.

She nodded. "I think there's science about that, too."

"Yeah, all the science," he said, recycling the words because the blood supply to his brain had diverted south.

She glanced up at the open book still raised above his head. "Oh my!"

He followed her gaze to an illustration of a woman strad-dling a man.

"Looks like we've got that one down," he said and instantly wanted to punch himself in the mouth.

She glanced up at the illustration. "I think there's more to it."

He nodded, lowering the book. "Right, they're naked from the waist down."

"Yeah," she breathed as their gazes locked, and then, the penny dropped.

Georgie tore off her cardigan and pulled off her blouse as he unbuttoned the first few buttons on his dress shirt then whipped the garment over his head.

"Wow!" she said, running her fingers down his chest.

"Christ!" he bit out, taking in her sexy as hell black bra and her perfect breasts. She'd done a damn good job of hiding her killer curves under that hideous outfit.

She reached to release her bun, but he stopped her. "Leave it. I like you like this."

For all the crap he'd talked about hating the messy bun hairstyle, on Georgie Jensen, it was downright alluring.

She bit her lip. "We need protection."

He held her gaze. "I've got a condom."

"I have them, too. An eight values safety."

"So does a ten," he countered.

"Where are yours? Back in your car?" she asked.

"No, in my wallet, in my pocket."

"Okay, you win. Mine are in my room."

He grinned. "I told you, tens always win."

She ran the tip of her tongue across her top lip in a sultry as hell move that kicked his desire into overdrive. "Shut up and take off your pants. Eights value efficiency and uninterrupted attention to the task at hand."

With speed second only to the comic book character, the Flash, he set the book on the table, shrugged down his pants and boxers, grabbed his wallet, and pulled out the condom.

"Tens go above and beyond, so you better be ready to have your mind blown."

"Talk is cheap to eights if you can't back it up," she challenged.

He tore open the packet and rolled on the condom as she watched. "Georgiana," he said in a low rumble.

"Yes?" she answered, meeting his gaze.

He ran his hand up her leg to the apex of her thighs, and she gasped as he dipped his finger inside her panties and found her...

Holy hotness!

"You seem to have a marked physical response to a ten," he said, feeling her sweet wet center.

"It's not for you. It's a marked physical response for...stress relief," she said, then gripped his cock. "Looks like you're in need of stress relief, too. Luckily, you've got an eight *on top* who can help you out."

He didn't care if she was on top, on the bottom, or strapped to the back of a Chrysler, he needed to have her, and he needed her right now.

He gripped her lacy panties. "You mind if I rip these off? I'd really like to start fucking your brains out. You know, for stress relief."

"Do it," she gasped, all wide-eyed and blushed cheeks.

He didn't need to ask twice. He tore off her panties like they were made of tissue paper, and the look of carnal hunger in her eyes made him want to rip a hundred more pairs off her fucking fantastic body.

Panty free, he gripped her hips and positioned her over his cock, weeping with desire. She sank down slowly, inch by delicious inch, their gazes locked as if they were in some crazy Kama Sutra trance.

This wasn't how he fucked. He was pretty much a take-her-from-behind kind of guy. This eye to eye thing was...*incredible*.

He blinked, lost in the sea of blue-green, as she wrapped her arms around his neck and rocked her hips.

"Georgiana," he whispered like her name was the answer to every question he'd ever had.

Georgie closed her eyes as if she were allowing his voice with her name falling from his lips to wash over her. He cupped her cheek. Was she always this pretty? He took in the light dusting of freckles on her cheeks and her lips that looked made to be kissed and nipped and sucked.

She opened her eyes. "Hey," she said gently.

He brushed his thumb across her bottom lip. "Are you okay? Is this all right?"

"I was kind of hoping there'd be some movement," she said with the dirtiest little grin he'd ever seen.

He matched her expression. "I wanted to give you a sec to prepare."

Her blue-green eyes darkened with desire. "Oh yeah?"

He nodded. "You better hold on. The earth is about to move."

A challenging glint sparked in her eyes. "You're that good?"

He caressed her ass, then squeezed the tender skin. "I'm a ten. Of course, I'm that good," he growled and pumped his hips.

Georgie rode his cock, rising and falling, as he controlled the speed and set a punishing pace. The friction between them ignited a firestorm, and she was fucking glorious. She arched into him, and he slid a hand between them and massaged her tight bundle of nerves.

"Jordan, it's so good," she moaned, her sweet cries driving him wild.

He captured her mouth, and their tongues met in a dance of lust and longing. Only a few hours had passed since he'd last kissed her, but she'd become like a drug, and he wanted more. Each lick and graze of her lips couldn't seem to satisfy his need. Heat swelled between them, intensifying their connection. His heart hammered in his chest as he got the best abs and cardio workout of his life, grinding and thrusting. And then, she was there, tightening around him. Her eyes blinked open, and in that second where she met his gaze, she owned him body and soul.

They flew over the edge, their mutual release surging

through them, pounding and throbbing as if they were surrounded by a hurricane, whipping their bodies into a sweaty, wet frenzy. And all he could do was inhale her vanilla scent and die a thousand carnal deaths, staring into her eyes.

She rested her head on his shoulder, and he wrapped his arms around her. But it wasn't just her body that he was holding close. It was the moment that felt like so much more than a little stress relief when their phones pinged simultaneously.

She tensed, and he knew why. She'd done just what he had, adding an alert to ring any time the Dannies posted onto their CityBeat blog. She lifted her head and glanced over at their phones on the coffee table.

"You did it, too?" she asked.

"Yeah, we need to know when they post."

Georgie glanced away. "Do you have an alert set for when I post?"

"Yeah, I do," he answered, hating that keeping tabs on her now felt like some weird kind of betrayal.

She nodded, more to herself than to him. "I have one for you, too."

Because here's what it boiled down to, like the Dannies, he was her competition, and she was his.

Their phones pinged again, and she lifted herself from his lap.

He removed the condom. "Where's your bathroom? I should take care of this."

She gestured toward a dark hallway. "Second door on the left."

Fucking hell! What had they done? He threw the tied-off condom in the trash, then cleaned himself up. Turning to leave, he caught his reflection in the mirror. It still surprised him how he always expected to see that skin and bones teenager and not the ripped athlete he'd become. He had so much more he wanted, no, needed to accomplish to keep putting miles between his old and his new life, and that started with winning the blog competition.

He left the bathroom and found her dressed and staring at her phone.

She glanced up at him. "The Dannies posted an amazing story to their blog about how instead of finding dates for themselves at the grocery store, they reunited two childhood sweethearts. Danielle wrote that she could feel the love pulling them together and that she and her brother served as a conduit to connect two people who still cared for each other while simultaneously making our world a better place."

He retrieved his shirt and put it on. While he and Georgie were screwing, the Dannies were winning.

He shifted his weight from foot to foot. "I better go."

She crossed her arms. "Yeah, I need to get to work on my post."

He gestured to the plates. "Thanks for dinner and the..."

And what? The fucking fantastic sex?

"The stress relief," she supplied.

He nodded. "Right, it was very...effective."

Dammit! Now he really did sound like the Emperor of Asshattery.

"We'll talk soon. We can start your race training," he added.

She chewed her lip. "Sure, it's a date. Well, not a date. It's an appointment."

He took a step toward her. What was he supposed to do? Give her a kiss on the cheek? The lips? A hug? But before he could decide on the right way to say goodbye to his competition, who also happened to be the best sex he'd ever had, Georgie thrust out her hand.

A handshake. How awkwardly perfect. But entirely fitting for how they had to behave from this point on. No more kissing demonstrations or Kama Sutra stress relief.

He left the bungalow and closed the door on not only Georgie and her shelves of books and her killer body, but a world where she could be his.

"You play to win. That's what Deacon would do," he whispered into the night air without even a backward glance.

"Are you telling us that, two days ago, you kind-of-accidentally-sort-of slept with Jordan Marks?"

Georgie cringed at hearing Becca repeat her admission and placed a tray of vegan chocolate chip cookies on the bookshop's counter. Becca took one then handed another to her sister, Irene, who'd stopped by to say hello. It was good to see her. Now that she was married to her eight and was not only bartending but also managing the Tennyson Bistro, they didn't see each other as much as they'd used to when she'd first opened the shop.

Georgie glanced between the Murphy sisters. If she were being honest, it was more like she'd ridden Jordan Marks like a Kama Sutra cowgirl while the two of them had harnessed enough orgasmic energy to power the city for a week, maybe even a month.

But she didn't need to go into that kind of detail—especially since it could never, ever, ever happen again.

Ever.

Ever, ever.

"Yes, I accidentally slept with him. But we only did it to

relieve the stress brought on by the competition. There's science and shit about it," she answered, then crammed an entire cookie into her mouth.

"Whoa, Nellie!" Irene said, grimacing at her vegan debauchery. "Go easy on that cookie. It's not Jordan Marks' cock!"

Becca pressed her hand to her lips and stifled a laugh.

Georgie took a giant gulp of water to wash down the treat. "You guys, it's not funny."

"It kind of is. I mean, how often do you hear about women accidentally falling onto a guy's dick?" Irene replied, biting back a grin.

"And, kind of sort of having your brain scrambled by crazy hot sex," Becca added.

Georgie wiped a crumb from her lip then gasped. "I didn't mention anything about it being crazy hot."

"Georgie, you walked around this bookstore smiling like an idiot and handing out cookies like a girl scout on crack."

"They're vegan!" she huffed. She shouldn't have even mentioned her stress relief session with Jordan.

"It's okay if you like him, Georgie," Irene said and swiped another cookie.

Georgie blew out a frustrated breath. "Actually, it isn't. He's my competition."

"How's that going? I haven't checked CityBeat yet today," Becca said, pulling her phone from her pocket.

The truth was, so far, it wasn't going well, at least, for her. Just as she'd thought, the Dannies' post about reuniting childhood sweethearts in the frozen pizza aisle had earned them a tsunami of likes. Jordan's post about the health benefits of honey and using it to meet a like-minded ten hadn't done great, but it had garnered more likes than her blog about vegetables bringing eights together.

"The Dannies are in the lead with Jordan in second place

and me in third," she answered. She checked the score every time nobody was looking.

"That was pretty cool how Daniel and Danielle just sensed those two people were meant to be together," Becca said, glancing at her phone. "And they just posted that the couple told them that when they decided to have kids, they'd name the baby after them."

Georgie straightened a row of books. "Did they post a picture of the happy couple?"

Becca stared at her phone. "Nope, it's just an article with a picture of a grocery store. But I'm not sure which market they went to. I don't recognize this shop."

Something seemed off. What are the chances of reuniting two lost lovers in under two hours? But Georgie shrugged off her skepticism. Harboring jealousy over the Dannies' amazing post wouldn't help her get ahead.

"What's on the schedule today? Any more accidental fucking?" Irene asked with a teasing glint in her eyes.

Georgie crossed her arms. She kind of accidentally sort of shouldn't have told her friends anything about her Kama Sutra antics. She mustered up the most neutral expression she could.

"Jordan's going to teach me how to run."

"You, the queen of meandering walks, is going to run?" Becca asked with a frown.

"A 10K race is the final event, and Jordan, the super trainer, is hellbent on me running in it. The past two days, he's sent me detailed workouts to help get my body into shape," she replied.

"Have you done them?" came a man's deep, rumbling voice.

The women shrieked and looked toward the door and found none other than the super trainer himself.

"Are you a spy or something? I didn't even hear you come in!" Georgie exclaimed, her pulse racing.

Jordan glanced around. "It's a bookshop. Aren't people supposed to come in?"

"Yeah, but most say hello," she shot back.

He gave her that damn toe-curlingly hot shit-eating grin. "Hello."

"Hello," she barked. She wasn't a barker, but just the sight of him made her want to rip off his clothes and try the next Kama Sutra position.

The trifecta held up their water cannon, and she derailed the hot and bothered train of thought.

"Did you do those conditioning runs I sent you?"

"Hell no! But I took a meandering walk," she answered.

Jordan sauntered toward the counter and clucked his tongue. "That's too bad. It's going to make today a lot harder for you." He turned to the Murphy sisters. "Hi there. I'm Jordan."

Crap! She'd forgotten her manners. Now it was her trifecta clucking their tongues at her.

"Irene and Becca, this is Jordan Marks. He works at that gym down the block."

They said their hellos, then Jordan took a step back and stared at Irene. "Have you been to Deacon CrossFit? You look familiar."

"There's no way—" Georgie began when Irene cut her off.

"Yes, you have a good memory. I dropped my husband off at the gym the other day. He's working with one of the trainers."

Jordan nodded. "Which one?"

"Sara," Irene replied.

"Sara's great," Jordan said, tossing her a little ha-ha glance.
Smug asshat!

Georgie waved her hands. "Hold on one hot minute. Irene, your husband is an eight. You met him following the Own the Eights method. He's not some musclebound meathead of a ten!"

Irene blushed and flashed the hint of a naughty grin. "He's still an eight. But now, he's an eight with washboard abs."

Washboard abs!

What was going on? Jordan Marks and his superficial Perfect Ten Mindset was seeping into every facet of her life.

She whipped off her apron then smashed another cookie into her mouth. "Let's get this over with," she said and headed toward the door.

"We'll hold down the fort!" Becca called.

"Have fun, but not too much fun!" Irene added.

She gave them a backward *screw-you* wave as she left the shop, seething about Irene's husband.

Jordan joined her outside on the sidewalk. "I can't believe that you're power-eating cookies before a run."

"They're vegan. It's like an energy bar," she answered, meeting his gaze when everything stopped.

The sweet lingering ache between her legs and the tingle of her lips wanting to be plastered to his were a powerful reminder that when it came to Jordan Marks, while her brain knew he was the devil, her body wanted to sin with this man all night long.

Jordan blinked as if he too had flashed back to their stress relief session. "Cookies are absolutely nothing like an energy bar. And I'll have you know that many energy bars might as well be classified as candy bars with the amount of sugar and…"

He glanced down at her feet.

"What?" she asked, checking out her Nikes.

"I've never seen you without your pilgrim buckle sandals."

She shook her head, then started walking. So, this was how it was going to be, which was a relief. She could play the part of a nerdy, well-read, environmentally conscious eight, and he could continue on as the reigning Emperor of Asshattery. But why did her mind keep flashing back to his eyes, hungrily devouring her body? Why could she still feel his hands gripping her ass?

Jordan caught up to her. "Since you said you were good at sprinting out of ballrooms, which sounds like the most insane form of cardiovascular exercise, let's start with that. Just pretend I'm that Brice Casey guy, and try to catch me."

The earth literally rocked off its axis.

Her jaw dropped. "What did you just say?"

Her trifecta gasped. Shit just got real.

He frowned. "I said, try to catch me."

She narrowed her gaze. "What did you say before that?"

Confusion marred his perfect ten face. "When I helped you catch your dog the other day, you kept calling me Brice Casey. I figured he was some guy who dumped you that you still had a thing for. You could draw on that energy for your sprint."

Heat rose to her cheeks. Fire stirred in her belly. If she were cast in a young adult paranormal movie, this would be the part where her hair would blow wildly in the wind as menacing storm clouds gathered behind her.

She took a step toward him. "I'm going to count to five. You better run, Marks. This is your first and last warning."

"You think you can catch me?" he asked with his signature smirk.

"One."

This asshat just unleashed World War III. Well, her version where nobody died.

He raised an eyebrow. "You, a meandering walker, think you can sprint as fast as someone who trains like an Olympic athlete?"

"Two," she bit out, unmoved by his rhetoric.

"This should be interesting," he said, now without the smirk and not quite so much swagger.

"Three."

He took a step back. "You're taking this very seriously, Georgiana."

"Four," she roared and raised her hands into the air like a sorceress calling the four corners.

"Holy shit!" he whisper-shouted.

Maybe her eyes had turned red like some evil super-villain or maybe her head twisted around like the chick in the *Exorcist,* but before she got to five, Jordan took off like a shot.

"Five," she whispered, channeling the drive of her Brice Casey scorn. Her vision narrowed, and she was off.

Legs pumping and arms slicing through the air, she focused on her mark, *Jordan Marks*, and blasted off the sidewalk. Jordan glanced over his shoulder as fear and disbelief flashed in his eyes. He picked up his pace, jumping over a yipping Pomeranian, then crossed the street and headed for the park.

Georgie sprinted, unfazed by the barking ball of fluff because there was no stopping her now. With the agility of a gazelle, a really pissed off gazelle, she closed in on him.

"You're such a Brice Casey!" she cried and lunged forward.

Grabbing onto his arm, her leg crossed in front of his, and they tumbled to the ground in a heap of gasps and yelps.

"Jesus Christ, Georgie!" he exclaimed, his back pressed to the ground.

She straddled him, like a hunter, prepared to wrestle her prey into submission. "Gotcha," she gasped.

His eyes as wide as saucers, he stared up at her. "That was crazy! Why'd you tackle me?"

Now, it was her turn to smirk. "You told me to pretend you were Brice Casey, and that douche canoe is the epitome of every jerk who thinks women are put on this planet to be an ornament on their arm."

"This guy really hurt you," Jordan said gently as something akin to shame or maybe remorse washed over his expression. He reached up and cupped her cheek in his warm hand. And, damn, if it wasn't exactly what she'd needed.

She took a breath and regained her composure. "Are you okay, Jordan? Please tell me I didn't injure the Marks Perfect Ten Mindset expert."

He chuckled. "Yeah, all five foot six inches of you really wrecked me."

But his eyes weren't laughing. Instead, they shined with concern.

He stroked her cheek with his thumb, and she was about to melt into the gentle touch of the asshat who could ruin everything for her, while at the same time, made her feel whole when a slow clap caught her attention.

She glanced up and raised her hand to shield her eyes from the sun, where two artificially flawless humans towered above them.

"Oh, Daniel, look how cute they are. They're like little puppies."

The Dannies.

Were they here for a challenge? She hadn't gotten a text.

"Georgie, we should get up," Jordan said, voice void of emotion.

At the sight of their main competition, he'd gone into battle-mode.

"Yes, you're right," she replied, scrambling off him and onto her feet.

"Are you guys out for a walk?" Jordan asked the Dannies, coming to her side.

The Dannies gave them matching pearly white smiles.

"We just finished..." Daniel began but stilled and looked to his sister, his dentist-approved smile faltering a fraction.

"Training a group of children with special needs," Danielle cooed without missing a beat.

"Right! Physical activity is so important no matter your age or ability," Daniel added.

Georgie glanced around the park. Except for a few parents pushing a trio of toddlers on the swings, there wasn't a child in sight.

"You understand the importance of exercise, right, Jordan?" Danielle queried smoothly.

Jordan crossed his arms. He was clearly no fan of the Dannies. His cool demeanor could be because of the competition, but she didn't quite get his extreme level of disdain.

"How nice of you both to care so much," he said with a thread of derision woven through his words.

Danielle fluffed her blond ponytail. "We do what we can. We love to post about our community service. It inspires our followers to be better people."

"That's so generous of you," Georgie answered, watching Jordan from the corner of her eye.

"It's the least we can do. We take our job as social influencers seriously," Daniel added.

"Yep," Jordan said as if *yep* were the exact opposite of what he really wanted to say.

She glanced up at him and then to the Dannies. Whatever his beef was, she wasn't about to get pulled into it. And shouldn't the Dannies be right up Jordan's alley? All shiny-happy-perfect-body people.

"I loved your post from the grocery store," she said, going for civility and getting a thumbs-up from her trifecta.

"The what?" Daniel asked and looked to his sister.

They did that eyeball thing again, and Danielle turned to her and turned up the wattage on her smile. "Such a happy coincidence that we were able to connect those two."

Okay, this was getting weird. Maybe their Danny brains were so crammed with perfect blog posts Daniel couldn't remember the Dannies' last post. But this was just a few days ago, and it was for a huge contest.

Danielle gave her the once-over and frowned. "Georgie, do you happen to know who's ahead in the Battle of the Blogs? Daniel and I have been so busy helping others that we haven't checked. And you probably have a lot of time on your hands since you don't seem to engage in any feminine grooming routines, which, by the way, I wrote about last week. You should really check it out. A few highlights and a little concealer could really go a long way for a girl like you."

Holy backhanded compliment! Now, she understood Jordan's cool demeanor.

She lifted her chin and schooled her features, going for an ice queen disposition. "You're ahead, but Jordan and I have some real zingers up our sleeves for our next blog posts," she said and met Danielle's gaze head-on. There was time for civility, and then there was a time for bringing the thunder. She tapped Jordan's arm. "Right, real zingers?"

"Yep," he said, this time like he meant it when a chorus of chimes pinged at the same time.

They all had their phone alerts set for the CityBeat texts.

Like a pair of rebooted robots, the Dannies took off without another word, and she pulled her phone from the band of her yoga pants.

"They sent an address," she said, reading the message, but Jordan didn't respond. She glanced up at him as he watched the Dannies disappear in a large SUV. She tapped his forearm again. "Those two are certifiable jerks, but you really don't like them, do you?"

He frowned. "I don't trust them. They're peddling supplements on their page, and their likes accumulate in batches."

She shrugged. "It could just be the way the CityBeat platform works, especially since the Dannies have so many followers. And I figured Danielle would be your type for sure."

Jordan cringed. "Why? Because she looks like a Barbie doll spliced with a Victoria's Secret model?"

"That's exactly why," she mumbled, wondering why the hell it bothered her to think of Jordan and Danielle as a couple.

"Appearance is just one component of being a ten, Georgie," he replied.

She glanced away. "Could have fooled me."

He blew out a frustrated breath. "Don't you see? Doing the real work to make yourself the best is what matters to a ten. Consistency and commitment are crucial. People can try to fake it, but it takes real dedication to be a ten in every facet of your life."

"You think the Dannies are fakes?" she asked.

"I think the Dannies are full of shit. That's why whatever the next challenge is, we've got to crush it."

We.

Why did that word send a flood of warmth crashing through her body?

She reached up and plucked a leaf and a few other pieces of greenery from his shoulder. "You've got a little grass on your shirt."

His expression softened. "You've got it all in your bun."

Her hands flew to her head. "I do?"

"Stop, let me," he said and combed his fingers through her hair.

For such a big guy, his touch was tender, just like when he'd kissed her.

He twisted a wisp of her hair between his fingers. "I know you hate everything about the Marks Perfect Ten Mindset, Georgie. But we need to work together to beat the Dannies. Whatever you think of me, they're ten times worse."

And what did she think of him? He was an asshat who poked

fun at her shoes and clothing. But he was also the same asshat who had rocked her world with the best kiss and the best sex she'd ever had, which she wasn't about to ever disclose.

She stared up at his perfect face. "Deal. Whatever the next challenge event is, we crush it."

GEORGIE

"This is not the kind of crushing it I was talking about," Jordan said under his breath as they drove up the bumpy gravel road. "Are you sure this is the right place?"

Georgie glanced out the windshield at the sprawling fields. They'd left the city and headed east where they'd traded highrises for hay bales.

She checked her phone's navigation app. "Yes, this is the right way. Maybe we're volunteering on a farm."

"Doing what?" he asked with a slight shake to his voice.

She shrugged. "I don't know. Whatever people do on farms. Maybe we'll milk cows."

"Do you see any cows?"

She didn't see much of anything until a house caught her eye.

"Hold on. There's something up there."

She leaned forward as a barn and a weathered farmhouse with a few cars parked haphazardly in a clearing came into view.

"We're probably doing a Habitat for Humanity thing, fixing up that old house. That would be in line with my Own the Eights philosophy for supporting the community. But I could be wrong. Don't forget, the CityBeat founders are known for doing publicity stunts."

Jordan frowned. "I'm getting a bad feeling."

"It's a farm. How bad can it be?" she threw back.

"Fucking hell," he muttered as he parked his BMW next to a Subaru splashed with the CityBeat logo.

Holy Farmer Fred! CityBeat was here!

"Look," she said and pointed to where Daniel stood, gesturing wildly, with a man and a woman she didn't recognize. She glanced around for Danielle and found her planted in the passenger seat of a giant black Escalade on the other side of the gravel lot. The other half of the Danny duo sported large dark sunglasses and sulked in her seat like a super diva.

She went to open her door. "Come on. Let's see what's going on."

"Do we have to?" Jordan asked, cutting the ignition.

"Yes, we have to!" she said, channeling Hermione's quasi-bossiness.

This was not the take charge, I'm-the-man-with-a-plan ten she was used to. Jordan looked nervous, which didn't make any sense. Then, the man startled at the sound of horses happily whinnying as if he'd heard the deadly roar of a lion about to attack.

They crossed the gravel lot and walked up to the trio, catching Daniel mid-rant.

"Danielle and I can't be here," he huffed. "We're allergic to horses."

A woman in a flowing blouse and yoga pants nodded. "You won't be interacting with the horses today. As you can see, they're in the barn."

Daniel shook his head. "Well, my sister's not getting out of the car. We need an alternate challenge."

"Sorry, dude," a young man holding a camera said and

shrugged his shoulders. "Hector and Bobby said there are no substitute challenges."

"Didn't you guys write a whole blog post about equine therapy?" Georgie asked, breaking into their conversation. She'd done a little internet reconnaissance on the Dannies last night, scrolling through their blog posts and trying to get a better feel for what she and Jordan were up against.

Daniel turned to her with a blank expression. "We...just found out about the allergy."

The horn on the Escalade cut through their conversation, and the group turned to find Danielle banging the steering wheel like a prizefighter going to town.

Holy Miss Temper Tantrum!

"I'm sorry, but we can't stay. We'll post something of our own," Daniel huffed then stormed off toward the black behemoth of a car.

No one said a word as the SUV peeled out and gunned it down the gravel road.

The man with the camera exchanged a glance with the woman in the flowing blouse. "Well, I guess it's just you two. I'm Barry, a producer for CityBeat. Hector and Bobby sent me to take photos and capture some video for the website from your goat yoga session."

"Goat what?" Jordan asked with a grave shake to his voice.

"Goat yoga," the woman said serenely. "I run classes here at my farm animal sanctuary. I hope you don't mind that it'll be a private session."

Georgie glanced up at Jordan, who'd gone completely white.

What the hell was wrong with him?

She smiled at the yoga teacher. "No, we don't mind at all, and personally, I've wanted to try goat yoga for years," she answered, ready to kick off her shoes and bust out a downward-facing dog while a frontward-facing goat chomped on the grass nearby.

112 | KRISTA SANDOR

The woman's expression grew introspective. "Practicing yoga surrounded by baby goats is a profoundly joyful experience."

"Baby goats?" Jordan rasped another shade paler.

"Could you give us a second?" she asked the yogi and the CityBeat guy.

Without waiting for them to reply, she grabbed Jordan's perfect forearm and pulled him over by the cars.

"What's going on with you? The Dannies just stormed off, giving us a chance to be featured on the CityBeat page. All we have to do is complete whatever they have for us here, and we should be able to catch up to them."

He swallowed hard. "I can't do it, Georgie."

She lowered her voice. "What do you mean you can't? You're the one who said we had to crush it. So, let's crush it. It's not a big deal if you aren't familiar with yoga. I'm sure the instructor will stick to basic moves, and you're as strong as a freaking ox. You have nothing to worry about."

A chorus of the cutest goat bleats echoed through the barn as a little herd of half a dozen baby goats followed the woman into a small gated area.

"Look at them, Jordan! This is perfect. We get to do yoga outside, harness our chi, and all while surrounded by baby goats!" she cooed.

He bristled.

Stupid Jordan! If anyone could ruin something as awesome as this, it would be him.

She pressed her fingertips to her eyelids. "I know it's not lifting a gazillion pound weight or doing a thousand pull-ups, but it's just yoga."

"It's not the yoga," he sputtered.

She dropped her hands to her sides. "Then, what is it?"

He released a slow breath. "I'm scared of goats."

Her jaw dropped. Who the hell was scared of goats?

She glanced into the fenced-off little goat haven. "Jordan, those are baby goats."

His throat constricted with another hard swallow. "Those freak me out even more."

She cocked her head to the side. "You're like twenty-nine times bigger than a baby goat. You could probably eat one of them in a single bite."

He shook his head. "I do not want to go in there, Georgie."

She schooled her features. It was time for some tough love. "You're going in there. You're the one who said we had to crush it."

He continued shaking his head. "I can't. One of my earliest memories is of being chased by a baby goat."

"Did you grow up on a farm?"

"No, I was little, like three or four, and my mom took me to a petting zoo. There was one asshole baby goat that knocked me down and tried to eat my shirt." He bristled. "I can still feel the damn thing tugging on the sleeve."

She had to turn this around. Crazy phobia or not, she needed him to complete this challenge. She glanced at the goats and pretended to study them carefully. "Listen, these do not look like asshole baby goats."

"How do you know?" he asked, eyeing them.

Total honesty, she didn't know the first thing about goats, asshole goats, or otherwise.

"We need to do this, Jordan. We need to beat the Dannies. I'll be right next to you. And if any of those baby goats try to eat your shirt, it's grilled goat chops for dinner. Any goat that messes with you will be toast or whatever goat food is called."

She crossed her fingers behind her back like a six-year-old who knew she was telling a lie. There was no way she'd hurt a baby goat, and she hated lying, but she hadn't gotten up that morning expecting to help a grown giant gladiator of a man overcome a goat fear. Whatever it was worth, this was the best she could come up with under the circumstances.

"Goat toast," he said and nodded to himself.

"Yes, goat toast. Just remember, the sooner we start, the sooner it will be over."

A baby goat bleated, and Jordan startled, then forced himself to take a slow breath.

"Okay, let's do this, but Georgie?"

"Yeah?"

"Do you promise to stay by my side?"

She smiled up at this hulk of a man who was terrified of baby goats. "Yes, I'll be by your side the entire time."

He reached out and took her hand into his. "Thanks, Georgiana. I mean it. I know this is kind of weird."

Kind of weird? Her trifecta covered their imaginary mouths, trying to hold back their laughter, but she no longer felt the urge to laugh.

She squeezed his hand and held his gaze. "You're going to crush it. I just know it."

He gave her the hint of a smile, and that little Brice Casey dimple on his cheek looked a lot less Brice Casey-ish.

"Do you guys mind if we get started?" the producer called, breaking into their goat pep talk.

The instructor waved them over to the gated area and directed them toward a pair of mats resting in the grass, while the producer took a few pictures of the animals.

"Let's begin in a seated position and settle into our surroundings," the yogi prompted.

Jordan sat down, crossed his long, muscled legs, and scanned the enclosure like a Navy Seal assessing a hostile target.

"Georgie," he whisper-shouted. "That one's looking at me."

She glanced over to see the sweetest baby goat who was, in fact, looking at him.

"Just close your eyes, breathe, and ignore them," she said, praying this man would not have a complete goat meltdown on camera.

But that baby goat was not going anywhere. It ambled over and sniffed Jordan's knee.

"What's it doing?" he whisper-shouted.

"Relax. It's just sniffing," she answered in an exaggerated singsong tone.

"Looks like Trixie has taken a shine to you, Jordan," the instructor said.

"The goat has a name?" he whispered with his eyes squeezed shut and panic lacing his raspy words.

"Trixie is a sweet name for a gentle goat," she said, begging the universe to make her statement true.

Georgie watched in horror as Trixie did a cute little goat hop and landed square in Jordan's lap.

"Okay, try not to panic, but the goat is kind of on your lap," she said and rested her hand on his knee.

He'd gone completely rigid. "I know. I can feel her little goat body."

"Time out," the instructor called, coming to her feet. "Looks like somebody is ready for lunch."

The woman walked over to a cooler and pulled out a bottle. "Here, Jordan. Trixie wants you to feed her."

His eyes popped open. "I have to feed the goat?"

Georgie gave him a plastered grin, hoping he'd play along and not freak out because the CityBeat producer had just switched from taking photos to filming.

"It's better than it eating your shirt, right?" she whispered back.

"I'll take that bottle," he said with renewed vigor.

Luckily, Trixie knew what to do. Extending her neck and resting it squarely in Jordan's palm, she latched on to the nipple and started sucking away. Jordan watched as the black and white goat went to town on the bottle.

"I'm doing it," he said with a wide punch-drunk grin, the fear in his voice replaced with wonder.

"You're doing great," she replied and scratched between Trixie's ears.

The producer knelt on the ground next to Jordan and Trixie. "I'd like to get some footage for the website. People are going to gobble this up."

"Just like Trixie's gobbling up her bottle," Jordan cooed.

He actually cooed!

He glanced over as Trixie neared the end of her lunch. "I'm crushing it, Georgiana."

With those four words, the Emperor of Asshattery disappeared. His green eyes sparkled with pride and relief. And when he looked at her, when he thanked her and patted the goat's little body, all she could see was his...*eight-ness.*

Yes, to her trifecta's disappointment, she'd decided to make this non-word a real word.

She parted her lips to say, say what? *You may not be the douche nugget I'd pegged you to be* when another precious black and white baby goat with a cute black ring around its eye hopped onto her lap.

"Oh!" she gasped as the tiny animal nuzzled up to her.

The yoga instructor handed her a bottle. "Looks like you're on lunch duty, too."

She shared a look with Jordan just as Trixie jumped off his lap, and another baby goat took its place.

"How are you doing?" she asked as the yogi handed Jordan another bottle and he went to work feeding baby goat number two like he was Farmer Fred.

He cradled the goat. "I'm good. I don't know if I've ever been better."

She nodded with the hint of a smile because the truth was, she'd never been better either.

"Four goats, Georgie! I fed four baby goats!"

Georgie sat back against the smooth leather seat and chuckled as they left the animal sanctuary and the scene of Jordan's great goat breakthrough. They hadn't done any yoga. Instead, they fed every goat, including the adult goats, all with the CityBeat producer documenting the event.

After two hours, the tally was in. Jordan had fed four baby goats, three adult goats, and hugged a lamb. A standard day for a six-year-old visiting a petting zoo, but a life-changing experience for a man with a farm animal phobia.

She watched him from the corner of her eye. The word handsome didn't even do him justice, and when he wasn't acting like a cocky bastard with that air of asshattery, he was absolutely lovely.

"I need to pull over," he said, all smiles and frantic energy.

She stared out at miles upon miles of farm country. "Here? In the middle of nowhere?"

"Yeah, I just need to—"

He cut off his sentence, hit the brakes, and pulled the Beamer onto the side of the road with a cloud of dust billowing behind them. He sprang from the car with the enthusiasm of a well-fed baby goat and took off toward a pond next to an abandoned-looking barn.

"Wait!" she called, running after him.

She found him at the edge of the water, staring out as the first drops of a gentle summer rain pebbled the surface.

He raised his hands like a Norse god. "You don't own me, goats! I'm not afraid of you."

If he weren't so earnest, this would be hilarious.

He spun around, and again, for the second time that day, took her hands into his. "This is huge for me."

She pushed aside the memory of those strong hands gripping her ass. "You should call your mom and let her know. I'm sure she'd be very proud of you."

His gaze darkened. "She would, but I can't call her."

"Why not?"

"She passed away when I was eleven," he said with the saddest smile that made her want to wrap her arms around him and never let go.

Tears pricked her eyes. "I'm sorry, Jordan. I didn't mean to..."

He shook his head. "It's okay. You're right. She'd be really happy for me."

Georgie felt a drop on her cheek, but it wasn't the rain.

"Are you crying?" he asked, releasing her hands and cupping her face.

She sniffled. "It's just very touching that you've overcome your fear of goats."

His expression softened. "And all thanks to you, Georgiana."

There it was. The low, sexy rumble of those four syllables that sent the butterflies in her belly into flight whenever he said her full name.

He stroked her cheek. "I probably reek of goat, but I really want to kiss you."

He could have been marinating in skunk spray. It didn't matter. She wanted it, too.

"I like the smell of baby goats," she answered and pushed up onto her tiptoes.

Their lips met, but this time, it wasn't the anger-infused Kama Sutra-inspired sexual melee that had erupted on her couch. This kiss was raw and honest. It spoke of weekends spent making love in a tangle of rumpled sheets and feather-soft pillows.

He pulled back and held her gaze. "Why does everything seem so possible when I look into those damn beautiful eyes of yours?"

Speechless. The girl who'd read thousands of books couldn't find the words to respond. Luckily, nature had a plan. The wind shifted as the sky darkened, and with a crack of lightning and the far-off rumble of thunder, the gentle sprinkling turned into a downpour. With rain trailing down his chiseled cheekbones like something out of a Hallmark movie, he led her into the old barn.

"Wait here," he said with a wide grin, then jogged back to his car.

What was happening? She trembled, and it wasn't from the cool breeze that had blown in with the storm. Stress. It had to be stress. She craned her neck and watched as he opened the hatch on the SUV, pulled out a blanket, then sprinted back to her.

"I've got—" he began, but she cut him off.

"Emergency supplies in your car just in case you get into an accident or are left stranded?"

He nodded.

She felt her cheeks heat. "Me too. It's just the kind of smart planning an eight would do."

"Or a ten, who has to be ready for anything," he countered.

"What are you ready for now?" she asked, her cheeks growing hotter.

He shook the blanket out and laid it on the ground. "You," he replied and guided her down next to him on the faded plaid quilt.

As gently as he held the goats, he removed her clothing. His touch left hot, tingling trails on her body where his fingertips brushed against her bare skin. Naked, and strangely, not at all embarrassed to be laid out in her birthday suit, Jordan pulled his shirt off, folded it carefully into a neat square, then lifted her head and slid the makeshift pillow beneath it.

His gaze ravaged her body. "Fuck me," he whispered, awe peppering the words.

She bit her lip. "I'm pretty sure that's what I'm about to do."

He kissed a line from her chin to her navel. "I hate to tell you this, Georgiana, but you've got the body of a ten."

She released a breathy giggle. "Don't let anyone tell you that you're not good at dirty talk."

"Eights like dirty talk?" he purred against her skin.

She closed her eyes as he worked his way lower and kissed her inner thigh. "This eight likes it when you say her name."

Had she said that out loud? She was prepared for him to give her crap about her admission, but he didn't.

He hummed a little laugh against her thigh. "Georgiana Jensen, you've been hiding one killer body under those hideous cardigans."

She threaded her fingers into his hair. She really should defend her love of cardigans, but it was hard to concentrate with the hottest guy on the planet planted between her legs.

"All I hear is blah, blah, blah, cardigan," she said in a breathy sigh.

"I think I'm about to hear *you* say *my name*," he growled before pressing a kiss to her sweet bundle of nerves.

"Oh, Jordan," she moaned as her ten went to work.

Did she like that he was right?

No.

But the man had a magic mouth that had her teetering on the edge, and that had to count for something.

She rocked against him, and he gripped her hips, setting a Marks Perfect Ten pace that had her crying out his stupid sexy name over and over again as she met her release.

He pushed up onto his elbows with a cocky grin. "You taste like..."

She tried to catch her breath, still bathing in orgasmic bliss. "If you say baby goats, I'm going to kill you."

He prowled the length of her body. "You taste like the last rays of sunshine at the end of a long summer day."

Oh damn! He could turn a phrase. Her traitorous trifecta swooned.

She ran her fingertips along his shoulders, feeling each taut, smooth muscle. "Do you have a..."

"Condom?" he asked with a naughty grin.

"Yes."

He shrugged out of his mesh shorts and pulled a foil packet from the pocket. "I'm a ten, Georgiana. I'm always prepared."

"Like a ripped boy scout," she said, watching this glorious man roll on a condom.

She was really about to own the eights—and then some.

He positioned his hard length at her entrance, then stilled, his body trembling.

"Are you cold?" she asked.

He shook his head. "No, it's you. You're..."

"An eight?" she teased.

Intensity burned in his gaze. "You're beautiful, Georgiana. Every part of you."

She wasn't expecting that, not from this ten, and could only answer by wrapping her arms around him. Their lips collided in a heated kiss as he thrust inside her, and the heat between them ignited. His sharp angles met her soft curves as if they were made for one another. They moved like lovers who'd been together for eons. He gripped her ass and changed the angle of penetration, and it was as if he knew what she needed before she even knew it herself.

"I could fuck you all day and all night and still not get

enough," he panted in tight hot breaths against her lips as he doubled his pace.

Dammit! He was good at dirty talk, too.

"Oh yeah," she breathed, the coil inside her tightening on the precipice of release.

"You smell so fucking good, like hippie vanilla bliss, and you're always so wet for me."

Crap! He had her there, too. It was like Kegel City the moment she laid eyes on him—that cavewoman part of her brain, ready to get down and dirty. Grinding his pelvis into hers, his ripped body never faltered from its pace. God help her, the shape this man was in, he could probably make good on that dirty talk promise and screw her brains out for hours on end.

But she wasn't going to make it that long. Unable to hold out a moment longer, her release tore through her body, spiraling, leaving her suspended between this world and the next.

"Fuck, yes!" he whispered in her ear as his pace ratcheted up a notch, and he joined her, flying over the edge.

In smooth, fluid strokes, he lengthened their pleasure. She rocked her hips against him as he held her close and their bodies wound down, slowly coming back from the crash of ecstasy.

He pressed up onto an elbow. "That was..."

Amazing. Mind-blowing. The best sex of her life. They'd totally be initiated into the Orgasm Hall of Fame. If that were a thing.

"Yeah, it was...," she answered, not sure why she couldn't say the words when their phones chimed.

He held her gaze with a torn look in his eyes. Did whatever they were doing feel like more to him? And holy crap, was it more to her? She couldn't go there.

"We should look," she said, trying to sound all business,

which wasn't all that easy with his hard length buried deep inside her.

He brushed a lock of hair from her cheek. "We should."

The phones pinged again, and he drew his fingertips down her jawline. Tender and so sweet, she wanted to surrender to his touch and close her eyes and forget anything besides the two of them existed. But she couldn't, and it wasn't her literary trifecta holding her back. This was something else. A needling in the back of her mind.

She schooled her features. "I don't bench press two-hundred-fifty-pound men for breakfast, so if we're going to get up and check what's on the CityBeat page, you've got to be the one who gets the ball rolling."

"You're right," he answered with a slight shake of his head.

He came to his knees. "I'm going to take care of this," he said and gestured to the condom.

She nodded then rolled over and grabbed her phone and gasped. "Jordan!"

"What?" he asked, finishing with the condom then pulling up his shorts.

"You! You're blowing up on CityBeat!"

He'd crushed it. The internet couldn't get enough of this gentle giant bottle-feeding baby goat after baby goat.

"How about you? What's your score?" he asked.

She scrolled to her blog. Her numbers had gone up, but not like his. "Not too bad for me," she lied.

He grinned down at her. "See, we've got this. Now stay put. I'll be right back."

"Where are you going now?"

"Back to the car to get an umbrella."

She frowned. "Why?"

He gave her the sweetest boyish grin. "It's still raining, and I don't want you to get wet."

She reached for her bra, suddenly feeling quite naked. "You don't have to do that."

"I want to."

She nodded, wishing the thread of disappointment running through her chest would disappear. "Okay, that will give me time to get dressed."

Jordan took off for the car when her phone pinged again. But it wasn't a CityBeat alert. She sucked in a shaky breath, then opened her email to find a past due notification.

"Shit," she whispered, staring at the dollar signs dotting the screen.

In a daze, she set her phone on the blanket and pulled on her clothes.

Jordan entered the barn, still sporting that wide grin. And why shouldn't he be smiling? He'd overcome his crippling goat phobia, got laid, and now had a bazillion more likes.

He glanced from her to the umbrella. "Would you like to grab some dinner on the way home?"

If she were a good eights girl, she'd say yes. In the course of the last couple of hours, this man had shown her his sensitive side, aka his goat phobia, rocked her world with not one but two orgasms, and ran out in the rain to get an umbrella for her. Everything screamed he was an eight, at least, for this afternoon. But her mind wasn't on the number eight. It was on all the numbers strung together, telling her how much she owed her creditors.

She picked up the blanket and began to fold it. "I should get home and work on my blog post."

He glanced out at the pond as thunder rumbled in the distance, and the air, once crackling with frenzied sexual energy, now hung heavy with the reality of their situation.

He crossed his arms. "You're right. We should get to work because..."

"Because it's a competition, and there'll only be one winner," she finished.

"Only one winner," he repeated as the warmth between them evaporated and was replaced with the cold hard truth.

They both wanted to be crowned the winner.

And if she wanted to keep her shop, that winner had to be her.

Jordan's phone pinged, igniting a spark of excitement, but he had to keep his cool, especially at the gym.

"Do you think that's CityBeat?" Deacon called from where he was eyeing Shelly at the gym's front desk.

"I'll check after I get the free weights in order," he answered, going for nonchalance, but it didn't work on his longtime mentor.

"Jordan?" he said with a smirk.

"What, Deac?"

"Your legs. You might as well be doing the pee-pee dance like my kids."

Jordan cocked his head to the side. "Aren't your twin girls eleven now? Kids don't do the pee dance at that age, do they?" he questioned.

Deacon had put all his energy into building his business. Jordan had always respected his mentor's dedication, but now, there was no reason for him to be visiting his gyms all over the state. Every Deacon CrossFit ran like a well-oiled machine. As Deac's number one trainer and the person in charge of setting up and monitoring all the locations, he was tasked with the day-to-day business. His boss should have plenty of time to see his kids, and maybe even try to patch things up with his ex-wife. Instead, the man seemed more intent on assessing Shelly's panty lines as she bent over and picked up the multitude of pens that mysteriously kept rolling off the desk.

"Are you winning?" Deac asked, taking one more look at Shelly.

"It's ongoing, and the numbers fluctuate, but we're within striking distance of being in first place," he answered.

Deacon frowned. "We? Are you talking about that gal they paired you with? I think that's bullshit. Every man *or woman* for himself."

"A slip of the tongue, Deac. I meant *I'm* within striking distance," he said over his shoulder as he took a little extra time with the weights.

"What's going on with that girl? She's not holding you back, is she?"

That girl. The one with eyes so captivating and a smile so damn sweet he couldn't think of anything else before drifting off to sleep.

He shrugged, choosing this as the perfect moment to slide into the mute, stereotypical gym meathead.

Georgie had barely spoken during the car ride back to Denver, and it had taken everything he had not to chase her down before she'd disappeared inside her bungalow when he'd dropped her off at home. It had been two long days since they'd made love in that barn with the rain as their backdrop, and they hadn't spoken once. Granted, they hadn't had any challenges. But Christ! Despite knowing they were competitors, he'd walked down the street to her bookshop half a dozen times over the last forty-eight hours only to chicken out and turn around.

He'd shot up on the scoreboard, and they were barely trailing behind the Dannies thanks to his last post, which

Deacon hadn't seemed to have read, most likely because the man was preoccupied with Shelly's ass.

Georgie's post about their goat yoga challenge, which didn't rake in many likes, left out his near barnyard meltdown and instead focused on the health benefits of adopting or simply interacting with animals regularly.

But he'd gone full baby goat confession.

He'd spilled his damn guts in his blog post and shared his childhood goat trauma. He'd waited for the *you're such a pussy* comments to flood in and for his subscriber numbers to drop, but the opposite had happened. There was a flood, but it was an outpouring of praise and shit-ton of likes on his page. It turns out, his goat phobia was a real thing. It even had a name, capra-phobia. Capra, Latin for goat. And there was also a foundation for kids who had been traumatized at petting zoos. He had mothers, fathers, farmers, yoga instructors, and psychothera-pists praising his admission and applauding him for taking steps to address his fear.

It was crazy. Guys bigger than him had started posting their fears of all sorts of weird shit.

For example, yo-yos.

Some dude in Kentucky was afraid of yo-yos. He commented that the goat confession blog post had inspired him to overcome his fear and hold a yo-yo. The guy even posted a picture of himself doing it.

In terms of the contest, it was the spike he and Georgie had needed. Now, thanks to those baby goats, they were only a handful of likes behind the Dannies, with him in second place and Georgie in third.

He wanted to be happy, and he was grateful his post had helped his Marks Perfect Ten Mindset followers, but he wanted success for Georgie, too. She was the only reason he'd made it through goat yoga without pissing himself from fear.

But his mentor was right. There could only be one winner, and Deacon had transformed him into a champion.

But fuck!

"Jordan, look at your damn phone!" Deacon called, stealing another glance at Shelly.

"All right, Deac. Don't get your panties in a bunch."

He pulled his phone from his pocket and opened the text.

"Well?" Deacon beckoned.

Jordan schooled his features, masking the surge of adrenaline that hit his system.

"I need to go. It's another CityBeat challenge. Are you good to close alone, Shelly?" he asked.

"I can stick around and help out," Deacon said, sharing a look with the desk clerk, who happened to be young enough to be his daughter.

A muscle twitched in his jaw. Fuck it! He didn't have time to cock-block his boss.

He headed to the locker room, changed into jeans and a T-shirt, then took another look at the text to double-check what he already knew.

CityBeat had texted him the address of Georgie's bookshop, but he sure as shit wasn't about to tell Deacon. He went through the back and jumped in his Beamer. If he'd left his car, Deacon, while probably already bending Shelly over one of the treadmills, would know something was up.

And why did CityBeat want him to go to the bookshop? Was he just supposed to pick her up? Was something going on at the shop?

He couldn't let his nerves get the best of him. He was Jordan Marks. The creator of the Marks Perfect Ten Mindset. He was cool under pressure, except for when it came to one particular woman in cork sandals and librarian glasses.

It took less than two minutes to get to her shop by car. He

parked, cut the ignition, then scrubbed his hands down his face. This was a competition. He'd go in. They'd do whatever the hell they had to do, and that was it.

But that wasn't it.

Get your head in the game, Marks.

He got out and walked up to the bookshop, and there she was, setting out a tray of muffins and doughnuts. Christ! What he'd do for her muffin.

Gah! Stop!

He opened the door, and she turned to him with a wide grin that immediately faded.

She narrowed her gaze. "What are you doing here?"

"CityBeat sent me. Didn't you get a text?"

She shook her head.

He pulled out his phone. Had he hallucinated? Had she been so prominent in his thoughts that he'd gone *One Flew Over the Cuckoo's Nest* and made it up?

No, it was there in black and white.

"The shop's closed. Our book club is about to start," she said, craning her head to look out the window.

"Who's in your book club?" he asked.

"A couple of spry octogenarians," she answered with a little smirk.

He tossed her a smirk of his own. "You don't think I know what octogenarian means."

She raised an eyebrow.

He shrugged. "Easy, it's a gathering of octopi."

She gasped, thinking she'd caught him being a dumbass.

He held up a finger. "I'm just messing with you. An octogenarian is a person lucky enough to live into their eighties. And I know that octopi isn't a real word. The plural of octopus is octopuses, but that just sounds like something you'd find on a porno site."

"That's right," she chuckled.

What the hell had gotten into him? His inner nerd hadn't reared its nine-dollar bowl-cut head in years. And why did she look so pretty with that damn messy bun, little denim capri pants, with you guessed it, those Birkenstocks, and that same cardigan over a white tank top? Was she like Mr. Rogers? Did she enter the bookstore and change into it every day? Did she sing a little bookstore *won't you be my novel* tune? It didn't matter. He'd grown fond of those stupid shoes.

He checked his watch. It was nearly seven thirty. "When do you start?"

She tugged nervously at the hem of her cardigan. "Around seven. It's strange for them to be late."

"What's the book?"

She glanced at the clock on the wall. "There's not just one book this time. We're doing our annual Jane Austen discussion. We'll talk about her novels, but tonight, we'll also dive into the parallels between Elizabeth Bennet's life in *Pride and Prejudice* and Jane's own life."

He picked up a book and mindlessly paged through it. "You're right, there are many similarities between their lives, like how Jane and Lizzie both grew up in busy, boisterous households. Except, Jane had brothers and a sister where Lizzie had only sisters."

He glanced up to find her looking like the cutest fish he'd ever seen, with her mouth opening and closing as if she wanted to speak but couldn't.

Look at that! It was usually his abs that rendered women speechless. With Georgie, his English degree did the trick.

"I..." she stuttered when the phone near the cash register rang. "Hold on," she said with a minute shake to her head.

He glanced down and noticed he was holding a paperback copy of *Pride and Prejudice.*

"Not bad, huh?" he said, speaking to the picture of the Bennet sisters on the cover.

He set the book down. What the hell was he doing? Was he talking to fictional characters in books now?

Georgie hung up the phone and sighed.

"What's wrong?" he asked, joining her at the counter.

"That was the husband of one of the women in the book club. He just told me that they're not coming."

"Why?"

"Michael Bolton."

"The singer, Michael Bolton?" he asked as his brows knit together.

Was that a legit reason to cancel plans these days?

She drummed her fingers on the counter. "Yeah, he's here in concert tonight, and they forgot to let me know they had tickets."

He scratched his chin. "There are eighty-year-old Michael Bolton groupies?"

She shrugged. "I hate to admit it, but who hasn't belted out the lyrics to "How Am I Supposed to Live Without You" in the shower?"

She did have a point.

"What happens now?" he asked when the door to the book-shop swung open, and a woman who looked like an older version of Georgie, wrapped in a fire engine red dress and drip-ping with diamonds, entered the room.

"Oh, Georgiana, pumpkin! I forgot how dank it was inside this sad little shop," the woman said, then removed a perfume bottle from her handbag and gave it a few sprays.

A hot blush bloomed on Georgie's cheeks. "What are you doing here, Mother?"

Mother?

"I'm here for book club, pumpkin. Didn't you say that City-

Beat would be here filming it? I told all the girls at the Denver Country Club that I was going to be on the web or the net or whatever they call it."

Georgie sighed. "I also told you that I don't know when they'll show up to film or take pictures."

The woman dropped the perfume back into her bag, then zeroed in on him, her cougar gaze raking over his body.

Holy hell! How was this woman not only related to Georgie but her mother?

Her stilettos clicked on the wood floor as she strode up to him. "You didn't mention Jordan was going to be here," she said, pawing his arm.

He took a slight step back. "It's nice to meet you, Mrs. Jensen."

This was getting a little awkward.

She waved a hand decked with gemstones. "I'm not Mrs. Jensen. I'm Lorraine Vanderdinkle. You might have heard of my husband, Howard Vanderdinkle. He's a venture capitalist. You know, tech, blah, blah, blah. I just can't keep up with it all."

He hadn't heard of Howard Vanderdinkle—and Christ, what a name! But he nodded politely, then glanced over at Georgie, who'd crossed her arms and plastered on the hard grin of one holding back sociopathic tendencies.

These two women couldn't be more different if they tried.

Lorraine turned to Georgie and huffed out an irritated sigh. "Shoulders back, pumpkin. Chin up. Don't you remember anything from our hard work during your beauty pageant days?"

The hot blush drained from Georgie's cheeks.

"Beauty pageant days?" he asked.

Lorraine gasped. "You didn't tell him?"

"That was a long time ago, Mom," Georgie said, piling a few books into a stack.

Mrs. Vanderdinkle—Jesus, he still couldn't get over that

name—feigned mock distress. "Yes, back when my daughter was a winner and not promoting this embrace of mediocrity with her *Eat the Sixes* blog."

"It's *Own the Eights,* Mom."

Lorraine gave another wave of her platinum-encrusted hand. "Whatever! Oh Jordan, she was such a knockout back then. We were killing it on the pageant circuit, and then, tragedy struck my poor beauty."

He looked from Georgie to her mother. "What happened? Did you get sick or hurt?"

"No, I got fat," Georgie answered over her shoulder, now busying herself by collecting all the snacks and refreshments she'd set out.

Lorraine shook her hands and scrunched up her face or at least tried. The woman seemed to have had a shitload of Botox.

"We don't use that word, Georgiana. I will not have it spoken in my presence." Georgie's mom pressed her bejeweled hand to her chest. "My beautiful Georgiana had become so unruly, Jordan. You should have seen what I had to deal with! She'd literally jump off the stage in five-inch heels and sprint out of the ballrooms where the pageants were held. And do you know where I'd find her?"

This was not a conversation he wanted to be a part of, but Holy Mary, it explained a hell of a lot about Georgie Jensen.

"I don't know," he stammered.

"Dunkin' Donuts," the woman said with the level of contempt usually reserved for drug cartel kingpins. "She'd tuck money into her dresses and costumes, even her bikinis, so she could escape and gorge herself with sugar and dough."

"God forbid that a child eat a doughnut," Georgie said, taking one off a platter and smashing it into her mouth.

Lorraine shook her head. "You should be like Jordan and those Dannies that you're up against, pumpkin. They strive to be the best. Isn't that right?" Mrs. Vanderdinkle asked as she squeezed his forearm.

He shared a look with Georgie, who had powdered sugar all over her lips.

"Well…" he began, not sure where the hell to start with this lady.

The Marks Perfect Ten Mindset was never about putting people down. His goal was to empower them. But before he could get that out, Lorraine pressed on.

"My dear friend Deidre Lockwood, from my Pilates class, has a connection to this blog battle. You must know the Lockwoods, right, Jordan?"

Nope, he had no idea. But again, he nodded politely.

"Well, she started taking those supplements the Dannies are promoting. What are they called? Oh yes, I remember. It's DannyLyfe Plus vitamins. Well, she got quite ill. But then again, she'd just been in St. Croix, and she could have picked up a stomach illness from bad shellfish. You know how it goes in the Caribbean."

He didn't.

Lorraine glanced around. "I do wish you'd let us at least buy you a less depressing bookstore. Then again, why run a business. How tedious! I keep telling you to come around when we're in Aspen. A few tech moguls might not mind…" Lorraine gestured to Georgie like she was a science experiment gone wrong.

Georgie's serial killer smile was back, and her mother looked away.

"Well, if I'm not going to be an internet star, I might as well meet the girls at the Ritz for drinks. Kiss, kiss, pumpkin," she said, then fluttered out of the shop, leaving a trail of Chanel in her wake.

Neither he nor Georgie said a word, but after what seemed like forever, or maybe forty-six seconds, he couldn't hold back.

"Holy fucking hell, Georgie!" he let loose.

She put up her hand. "Do not say one more word, Jordan."

"But that—"

She gave him a look that could stop traffic, and he mimicked zipping his lips when their phones pinged.

A challenge. But what kind of headspace was Georgie in?

She glanced at her phone and confirmed what he already knew. "It's CityBeat. They sent an address."

He nodded. "I can drive. I'm parked around the block."

She ran her hands down her face. "Okay, but we're not going to talk about what you just learned."

That you used to moonlight as a beauty queen?

He was still trying to wrap his mind around this book nerd, dropping the Moses sandals and strutting down a runway in five-inch heels. But...she did have a killer body, and she was pretty in that *I just rolled out of bed* sort of way. And then those eyes. Still, he couldn't picture her all primped and polished.

She locked up the shop, and they headed to the location, which happened to be downtown in a hip, young area sprinkled with bars, bistros, and microbreweries. It was Saturday night, and the place was already hopping.

"What do you think the challenge is?" he asked as they stared at a green awning with McGuire's Pub and Tavern written in bold letters. It was one of the largest bars downtown and had earned a rowdy reputation. Not his scene, but when he'd overheard a few clients recounting crazy nights on the town to their trainers, they always seemed to include this place.

"It's probably not goat yoga. Do you have a beer phobia you need to tell me about?" she deadpanned.

This woman!

"I do not have a beer phobia...that I know of," he replied matter-of-factly, hoping to make her smile.

It didn't. She gave him a distracted nod, barely even acknowledging his answer. This was not a good sign. That brief encounter with her mother had really done a number on her.

They sat quietly and watched as a stream of raucous men and giggling women, sporting tiny jean-shorts, entered the sprawling pub.

"Then we should be fine. We'll harness the Marks Perfect Ten Mindset. Always finish and always win. Rah-rah," she answered robotically.

He took her hand and gave it a squeeze. "Are you going to be all right?"

In the space of a breath, her neutral expression morphed into a smile with a wattage so high, he squinted.

"Smile like it's your birthday," she said as if she were auditioning for a teeth-whitening commercial.

"What are you talking about, Georgie?"

Her gaze grew distant. "That's what my mom would always say before I had to hit the stage and parade in front of the judges."

"It's not your birthday, is it?" he asked.

"No," she answered in one numb syllable.

He brushed his thumb over her knuckles. "Then I say smile however you want. Or don't smile at all."

She glanced over at him, sighed heavily, then pulled her hand from his, and got out.

"Do we have a plan?" he asked, walking a step behind her, but she didn't reply.

They showed their IDs to the bouncer then entered the sprawling bar. Music blared over the speakers while people stood in large groups, drinking and horsing around. It was wall-to-wall, hormone-infused twenty-something pandemonium.

"Jell-O shot?" a woman asked with a tray teeming with the frat house staple.

Georgie scooped up six mini-cups and popped the gelatin squares into her mouth as if they were Gummy Bears.

He leaned in toward the waitress, whose jaw had dropped. "What's in those?"

"Everclear. You know, one hundred ninety proof grain alcohol. And she just pounded six of them!"

Dammit! That was not good.

They weaved their way deeper into the bar and walked into what looked like a scene out of a *Girls Gone Wild* video. An elevated makeshift walkway pierced the center of the bar, running nearly the entire length with...holy fuck...young women in wet white T-shirts parading down the catwalk.

He gripped her shoulder. "Georgie, we don't have to stay here."

She blinked slowly, the Everclear clearly hitting her system, when she looked at one of the bar patrons and gasped.

"Virginia?" came a man's slurred voice from over his shoulder. He turned to see a decent-looking guy holding a beer with a *Daddy bought me this Porsche* haircut and a drunk grin on his face.

"It's been ages. You look...the same," the guy said, then took a sip of his beer.

Georgie stared at the man as if she'd seen a ghost.

"Sorry, dude," the man continued, then extended his hand. "Brice Casey, Vice President of Operations for Casey Pest Control."

Brice Casey.

This was the asshat who hurt Georgie.

Brice glanced around. "Good to see you, Virginia. I'm going to go check out the hot chicks on stage now," he slurred, then disappeared into the crowd gathered at the base of the runway.

As much as he wanted to go punch Georgie's jerk into next week, after what she'd endured in the last hour, he needed to get her the hell out of there.

He ran his hand down her arm. "Come on. Let's go."

She gave him a tipsy smile then glanced at the stage as a woman did a sexy spin, teetering on sky-high heels with her breasts on full display beneath her wet shirt, as the crowd roared with approval.

Georgie pointed to a group of women sitting at a table. "I'm going to go talk to those girls for a sec. I'll be right back."

He glanced at the attractive young ladies who each fit the bill for a Marks Perfect Ten woman, which now sounded like a pretty dick description for any woman. Were they friends of hers? He kept her in his line of sight when another voice called out.

"Jordan, I'm so sorry."

Barry, the CityBeat producer, pushed past a group of men. "We screwed up and got the dates switched around."

"What do you mean?"

"We meant to send you to trivia night," the man answered, hanging his head.

"Are the Dannies here?" he asked.

Jesus, that's all he needed!

Barry frowned. "No, and I think something is going on with them. They keep posting all this great content to their blog and getting tons of likes, but they're hard as hell to pin down."

Jordan nodded. At least, that was one thing off their plate.

Barry looked past his shoulder. "What's Georgie doing?"

"Talking to some friends," he answered, gesturing absent-mindedly toward the table while trying to figure out how he was going to get his former beauty queen out of there.

"Are you sure about that?" Barry asked with a perplexed expression.

He turned and scanned the crowd for a woman with her hair in a messy bun, wearing a cardigan. Instead, he looked on in horror at the back of a woman with killer curves, borrowing a pair of scissors from the bartender.

Georgie?

Her dark hair fell in sexy waves as she used the scissors to cut off the jean capris. Her firm ass cheeks peeked out from beneath the frayed denim that led down her long, toned legs. She returned the scissors to the bartender then sauntered over to the table with the women. He took a closer look at the table and cringed. Littered with the tiny cups containing the potent little squares, the women looked as if they were competing for the title of most Jell-O shots consumed in one evening.

One of the ladies passed Georgie a shot, and she joined the women as they swallowed their respective gelatinous cubes of highly potent alcohol.

As he and Barry looked on, Georgie gestured to her sandals and then to a pair of red heels lying on the floor next to one of the women. Beyond tipsy, the women laughed and swapped shoes, and Georgie slipped on the sexy heels effortlessly. Then, the woman dug into her purse and handed Georgie a small makeup bag.

He still hadn't seen her damn face yet and couldn't hear what they were saying. What the hell was she doing with these people? But he didn't have to wait long to find out. Sporting those fuck-me heels like she was born to wear them and her face now made up with red lipstick and black eyeliner, the book nerd with a bun turned, transformed into a smoking hot vixen, rocking every curve.

He glanced over at Barry, whose jaw might as well have been on the floor.

Georgie glided over, hips swaying with each step. "Good! You're here, Barry. You're going to want to get this on camera."

"Georgie," Jordan uttered, finding it hard to form words. She was always pretty, but this new Georgiana Jensen was a full-on sexpot temptress.

She patted his cheek. "Buckle your seatbelt, Marks. I'm about to school you on what a perfect ten really looks like."

He shook his head. "You don't have to do this."

Anger, disappointment, and determination flashed in her blue-green eyes as she set her cardigan on the bar, then swiveled on her five-inch heels and made a beeline for the DJ booth.

"She's really going for it. We should get to the stage," Barry said, holding up his phone to get some footage.

It was like watching a car wreck in slow-motion. Georgie, now wearing only a white tank top, barely-there jean shorts, and sexy red heels leaned over and spoke to the deejay presiding over the wet T-shirt contest. The man, grinning like a fucking idiot, handed her a bottle of water, and she climbed the steps to the stage.

"We've saved the best for last! Let's welcome Georgiana to the stage!" the DJ crooned over the microphone as Warrant's heavy metal hit and unofficial stripper ballad, "Cherry Pie", blasted from the speakers and the crowd went wild.

A spotlight illuminated Georgie in a golden glow as she held up the water bottle and threw the crowd a sexy little smirk, which ratcheted up the boisterous group.

"That chick's hot as hell, right, dude?"

Jordan glanced over to find the asshat, Brice Casey and anger surged through his veins.

A muscle ticked in his jaw. "If it takes a wet T-shirt contest for you to see Georgiana's beauty, then you never deserved her," he bit out, and before he could stop himself, he took the beer from the moron's hand and dumped it on his head.

VP of Pest Control, take that!

"What the fuck? If you weren't as big as a tank, I'd totally kick your ass," Brice whined, brushing the liquid off his shirt as he turned and headed for the restrooms.

Jordan didn't hold back a grin as euphoric victory replaced his anger until he glanced at the stage to find Georgie tipping the plastic bottle. Water drenched her white tank top, revealing her gorgeous breasts and torso. Rivulets trailed down her legs, and she might as well have been every wet dream he'd ever had. Except, this was Georgie Jensen. She wasn't a vixen exhibitionist. She was a sweet woman with a good heart who loved literature and helping others.

"Let's see it, Georgiana! Show us what you've got!" the DJ bellowed.

In time with the music, Georgie strutted down the catwalk as if she owned it.

"Jesus, Mary, and Joseph," Barry rasped as Georgie made her way toward them.

She moved like a supermodel, devouring the stage, but she wasn't smiling. Not even close. Her expression had gone blank as if she'd disappeared inside herself. Was this how she'd survived years on the pageant circuit?

Men banged their hands on the catwalk as she passed them. A glass beer bottle someone had left on the stage tipped over and rolled toward the center of the runway.

And Georgie didn't see it.

He burst through the crowd, pushing the rowdy, hooting men out of the way just as her heeled foot collided with the rolling bottle. She pitched forward, and he caught her flailing body in his arms.

"Wow, man! Good save!" Barry said, still filming.

Georgie wrapped her arms around his neck as shame flooded her gaze.

"How about we get out of here?" he asked gently.

The realization of what she'd just done was written all over her face, and she blinked back tears.

"Yes, I'd like to leave," she said, tightening her hold.

The crowd parted as he carried her through the bar and out the front door into the cool night air.

She rested her head on his shoulder and sighed heavily. "You can set me down now."

He complied, but as soon as her feet hit the ground, she wobbled, and he caught her forearms.

She leaned into him. "I'm not really a big drinker. I think those Jell-O shots were pretty strong."

He wrapped his arms around her and pulled her close. "Yeah, you don't want to mess around with Jell-O shots."

She nestled in against his chest as relief washed over him. He was so damned grateful to have her off that stage and in his arms.

He rested his chin on the top of her head. "Can I ask a favor of you?"

She chuckled against him. "You did save me from an awful fall. A favor is the least I can do."

He tightened his grip on her wet, shivering body. "Give me a heads-up next time you decide to unleash mayhem in a bar."

She shook her head against his chest. "Did I really just enter a wet T-shirt contest?"

"And you won it."

They pulled apart to find Barry, holding a trophy of a naked Barbie doll fixed to a solid wooden base.

He handed her the fucking offensive prize.

"You know I have to turn in the footage to Hector and Bobby," he said, not meeting either of their gazes.

She nodded. "I know it's your job, Barry. I understand."

"Thanks, Georgie," the man answered with slumped shoulders. He started off down the street then turned around. "Are you guys going to be all right?"

"Yeah, Georgie and I will be fine," he answered, pressing his hand to her back and wishing she was still in his arms.

After Barry was out of sight, Georgie took a wobbly step forward. "I think all those Jell-O shots are really kicking in."

"Seven will do that. Let's get you some coffee," he said as his phone rang.

He wrapped an arm around her, then pulled out his phone. "Shit, I need to take this."

"Go ahead," she said with a woozy grin.

He pressed his cell to his ear. "Hey, Uncle Rob, what's up?"

"Did you forget what day it is, Jordy?"

Jordan closed his eyes. Dammit! With all the CityBeat commotion, he'd forgotten.

"He's here. He's drunk, and he's not leaving," his uncle continued in a weary voice.

"I'm sorry. I'm on my way," he answered and shoved his phone back into his pocket.

"Is everything all right?" Georgie asked.

He held her gaze. There was no way he was going to leave her alone tonight, not after what she'd gone through.

He tucked a lock of hair behind her ear. "We're going on a little drive. There's something I need to take care of before I bring you home."

10

Jordan pulled into a parking space next to an old F150 pickup in the potholed lot and cut the ignition. He glanced from Georgie, sleeping peacefully in the passenger seat, to the structure in front of them. Another bar that had the potential to be more explosive than the last one. But this rundown place wasn't in Denver's trendy downtown. No, this bar was forty miles due east of this city in the tiny Colorado plains town where he'd grown up. A prickling sensation spider-crawled down his spine. No matter what he did, no matter where he went or how he'd changed, this place would always be a part of him.

He patted her leg. "Georgie, we're here."

"Where's here?" she yawned, opening her eyes.

"My uncle's bar."

She cringed. "I don't think I should drink any more tonight."

He stared at the familiar brick building. "We're not here for drinks. We're here to get my dad."

She sat up. "Your dad?"

He glanced at the paper cup, resting in the car's console. "Yeah, you downed all that coffee, and then you were out like a light. I'm sorry I didn't get a chance to explain. But my dad's in there, and he's not doing very well. I need to get him home."

"What happened?" she asked, now fully awake.

Jesus! Where should he start? The part where his mother died eighteen years ago, and his father became the worst version of himself? Or should he fast-forward to the part where the man berated him for being skinny and weak and ridiculed his love of books and comics, wishing he'd favor baseball and muscle cars instead?

He decided to go for a more direct answer. "Today would have been my parents' thirty-second wedding anniversary. Since my mom's death, he hasn't handled this day very well."

She rested her hand on his arm. "I'm sorry, Jordan."

He glanced at the building, not wanting her to see the shame in his eyes. "I usually drive up and make sure he doesn't drink himself into a stupor. But with everything going on, I blanked it out this year. This is my uncle's bar. He's the one who called."

"What can I do to help?" she asked with so much kindness infused into the words that alone nearly broke him.

He steadied himself. "Nothing. In fact, just wait here. I'll go in and get him."

She unbuckled her seatbelt. "No way. I'm going in with you."

"I can do it alone, Georgiana."

She gave him that sweet smile. "Well, tonight, you don't have to," she answered, then glanced from the paper cup to the building. "And...I could really use the restroom."

He chuckled. "All right, but I've got to warn you, my dad's a little rough around the edges even on a good day."

She pursed her lips. "Jordan Marks, you met Lorraine Vanderdinkle today. If there's anyone on the planet who can understand what it's like to have a difficult parent, it's me."

He wanted to kiss her. He wanted to forget about his father, press his lips to hers and shut out everything. His hometown.

His emerging doubts about Deacon. The contest. If he were a magician, he'd make it all disappear. But he wasn't. He was just a man who had to bring his long-grieving father home, and the part of him, that awkward kid who'd lived through years of bullying, was glad she was here with him.

"Okay, once we get inside, the restrooms are down the hall on the right. Look for the jukebox, and you can't miss them. I'll head to the bar and work on getting my dad to leave."

"Sounds like a plan," she said with that same sweet smile.

Here goes everything.

His pulse kicked up as they entered the bar. Georgie left his side and headed down the hall while he scanned the barstools. It wasn't hard to find his dad. Only a few men still lingered over their lagers, and it was easy to spot his father's large frame hunched over a beer with a few empty shot glasses stacked in a neat row.

He glanced down to the other side of the bar to where his uncle leaned against the polished counter, chatting quietly with a couple of men, and caught the man's eye. His uncle gave a furtive look toward his father, then shook his head.

This wasn't good.

All the bar patrons seemed to have migrated as far as they could to get away from his father. His old man looked like the stereotypical lone wolf, dark, foreboding, and isolated. The door to the restroom slammed shut, and knowing he only had a few moments before Georgie returned, he started toward his father when the man lifted his head, sensing his presence.

"I should have known Robbie would reach out to you," he bellowed without even turning around. "It's too damn bad that it takes a call from your uncle to remember the woman who gave birth to you."

A muscle ticked in Jordan's jaw, and red-hot anger surged through his veins. There wasn't a damn day that passed that he didn't think of her. Her twinkling laugh. Her wide smile. Cuddling in his bed, listening as she read his favorite books aloud. His father had taken the sudden passing of his wife hard. Damn hard. They'd had two weeks with her between her terminal diagnosis and her death. But what the man hadn't considered, in his unspeakable grief, was that his son was hurting, too.

"Pop, it's time to call it a night," he said, working to keep the emotion out of his voice.

"It's time when I say it's time, Jordy."

Jordy.

When his mother used to call him that, it rang with love. With his father, anger oozed from each syllable.

"Come on. Uncle Rob needs to close up soon," he tried again.

His father waved a hand toward the end of the bar. "I don't see your Uncle Rob asking any of those sons of bitches to go."

This mean drunk wasn't his dad. Sure, the man had become distant and hardened over the last eighteen years. But he only drank like this on the one day that was too painful to face without Jack Daniels by his side.

"Please, Pop," he coaxed.

"Time to go, huh?" his father replied, and Jordan breathed a sigh of relief. Could it be this easy?

He got his answer when his father sprang up, sending the barstool skidding across the floor, and stood nose to nose with him.

A damn Marks family standoff.

"I'm the one who decides when I'm good and ready to leave," his father hissed.

He held the man's gaze, unflinching when the unmistakable synthesizer intro of "How Am I Supposed to Live Without You" by freaking Michael Bolton cut through the confrontation.

He looked over his shoulder to find Georgie, smiling and coming toward them.

His father gave her the once-over and frowned. "Did you bring a hooker along to pick me up?"

Georgie laughed and shook her head. "Sir, I'm not a hooker. I recently ingested seven Jell-O shots then entered a wet T-shirt contest as a result of poor judgment and deep-seated issues with my mother. I actually own a bookshop. My degree is in library sciences."

His father's hardened expression softened. "If bookshop owners look like you, I might start reading."

She extended her hand. "I'm Georgie Jensen, Jordan's friend. It's nice to meet you, Mr. Marks."

"Dennis," his father sputtered. "My name is Dennis, but some people call me Denny. That's what my wife used to call me."

She gave his father that sweet, wash-away-the-pain, Georgie smile. "Then, Denny, it is."

His father grew pensive. "I do need to ask you something, Georgie."

"Anything!" she chirped.

His old man narrowed his gaze. "You really found this song on the jukebox?"

She nodded, her grin dialing up a notch. "Yeah, isn't it great?"

His father turned to the men congregating at the end of the bar. "You've got Michael Bolton on the jukebox?"

"He's a national treasure," a small man on a barstool said, raising his glass.

His uncle shrugged. "He kind of is."

"To Michael Bolton! May we all relish in his lyrical wisdom," Georgie added, pretending to raise a glass.

Jordan glanced around, and to his astonishment, everyone

began clinking beer steins. His dad even pretend-clinked with Georgie.

"Denny, can we take you home? And once there, could I possibly borrow a T-shirt? This isn't my usual Saturday night attire."

"Jordy's got drawers full of T-shirts up in his room. I'm sure we can set you up with something, right, *son*?"

Son.

Disgrace and disappointment used to permeate that word when it fell from his father's lips. Tonight, it sounded like it used to when his mom was still with them.

He nodded because he couldn't speak. Not unless he wanted to unleash a barrage of squeaks and sobs, and that sure as hell wasn't an acceptable Marks Perfect Ten response.

Georgie turned to go when his father rested his hand on her shoulder. "Would you mind if we stayed until the song ended? That Michael Bolton really has a voice," his dad said, grinning at Georgie.

She matched his smile. "Only if you sing it with me, Denny."

Jordan caught Georgie's eye, and she threw him a quick wink. Emotion welled in his chest as his burly, hard-edged father parted his lips and belted out the ballad's refrain.

Jordan climbed the stairs to his childhood bedroom, tracing his fingertips along the familiar grooves in the railing, and knocked on the door.

"Can I come in?"

"Yeah, I'm decent," Georgie answered.

He entered his room to find her wearing his worn Superman T-shirt and perusing his bookshelf.

She looked over her shoulder. "Is your dad asleep?"

He entered the room and took in the faded comic book posters on the walls and the plastic glow-in-the-dark stars his mother had helped him stick to his ceiling on his tenth birthday.

"Yeah, he likes to conk out in front of the TV. He's slept in his recliner since my mom died. I got him settled, turned on the Home Shopping Network, and he was out like a light."

She glanced down at the Superman shirt. "I hope you don't mind."

He shook his head. "I'm glad you found one that works—and you can never go wrong with Superman."

Her gaze flicked to his top dresser drawer, and his heart dropped into his stomach. "You saw them."

"I didn't mean to. I was just looking for some shirts."

He went to the dresser, pulled out the drawer, littered with straws and photographs of a skinny, awkward, Jordy Marks. His pulse slowed, and strangely, relief washed over him.

"I wasn't always a Marks Perfect Ten kind of guy. At eighteen, I was six four and barely one hundred sixty pounds wet," he said, touching the corner of his high school graduation photo.

She stood next to him, her shoulder brushing against his arm. "Why do you have so many straws?"

"That's what the kids used to call me."

She frowned. "Straws?"

"Yeah, it started in middle school. All the douchebag jocks would steal them from the cafeteria. They'd stuff them in my locker and throw them at me in the lunchroom." He picked up two straws and proceeded to make them walk. "They teased me and said I walked like this. The morons weren't clever enough to come up with anything better."

Concern shined in her eyes. "That couldn't have been easy to endure, but why'd you keep them?"

He stared at the frayed white paper wrapper. "I don't know. Maybe because I needed them to be just straws, and not me."

She took the straw from his hand and peeled back the paper, then smiled up at him. "See, you're right. It's just a straw."

He cupped her cheek in his hand, gazed down at her, and couldn't remember what life was like before this blog contest started. Everything centered around this woman, this embracer of the eights.

A little frown pulled at the corners of her mouth. "Can I show you something?"

"Sure," he answered.

She pulled a slim wallet from her pocket then sat down on the end of his bed. "You have to promise not to laugh."

He joined her. "I promise."

She nodded to herself, then slipped a photo out from behind her driver's license and handed it to him.

He gasped. "Holy hairspray! That's you?"

She plucked the picture from his hand and pressed it to her chest. "You said you wouldn't laugh."

"I'm not laughing. It's just..."

Georgie glanced at the image of a young girl with enough makeup spackled on her face to outdo the most dolled up newscaster by a mile.

He leaned in. "What's the sash say?"

"Little Miss Cherry Pie. It was for some pageant at a cherry festival in Michigan."

He tried to hold it together, but when he caught her gaze, they broke out laughing.

"You really did that "Cherry Pie" song justice tonight." He snorted, trying to hold back a full belly laugh.

"I never realized how really dirty little miss cherry pie sounds," she said through a bout of giggles.

"Georgie, that's awful, but at the same time, so freaking awesome."

"Shut up," she said with mock incredulity, then punched him in the arm.

Jesus! It stung. She was stronger than she looked.

Laughing, he fell back onto the bed, and she joined him. They stared up at the ceiling as the giggles subsided and a peaceful quiet set in as they stared up at the plastic replica of the big dipper.

"Jordan?"

"Yeah?" he answered, savoring the calming sound of her voice.

She rolled onto her side and propped up onto her elbow. "What would you do with the prize money if you won?"

He watched her closely. "I want to start my own gym."

Her brows knit together. "You're not happy at Deacon CrossFit?"

Was he happy?

"Deacon has been really good to me, almost like a second father. I met him when I was just starting college, and he took me under his wing. He not only helped me transform my body but my mind. I'll always owe him. I'll always be grateful to him."

She cocked her head to the side. "I feel a *but* coming on."

He chuckled. "But, I want to open a gym, my own business, that encompasses more than just pumping iron. I'd like to develop a nutrition program and keep putting out guided workouts people can do at home."

She smiled down at him, and he gasped as an idea sparked.

"What is it?" she asked.

"And I want to help kids who are bullied about their bodies. I could offer classes to children, teens, and young adults to not only help them get in shape but to also help them build self-esteem and confidence."

"Wow," she replied with a sweet smile as the dim lamp in the corner of the room cast her face in a warm glow, highlighting those captivating blue-green eyes.

"What about you? What would you do with the money if you won," he asked.

"You mean *when* I win," she corrected with a teasing smirk.

He rolled his eyes, and she laughed, but after a moment, her expression grew thoughtful.

"I'd sink most of the winnings into the bookshop. I've fallen…" She paused, and her throat constricted as she swallowed. "I mean, I'd like to expand the shop and add a children's area."

He reached up and wrapped a lock of her hair around his finger. "You can run storytimes for little kids and demystify Jane Austen and Shakespeare for the teenagers and I can teach them how to exercise and follow a healthy diet."

A dreamy expression lit her features. "It would be great if we both could win."

He stared up at the plastic stars and nodded. The strange thing was, he felt as if he already had.

A slice of comfortable silence stretched between them. She felt it, too. She had to. Whatever it was between them, it was real.

He turned to her. "Did you make an Own the Eights soul mate list?"

Her little smirk was back. "You've been poking around my blog."

"Maybe just a little, but I'm curious. You've helped thousands of people meet their eight. I figured it had to be more than just finding a guy in a Save the Whales T-shirt."

A sweet blush graced her cheeks. "Don't remind me. I haven't looked at a cucumber the same ever since that day."

"So, yes or no, Miss Georgiana Jensen Own the Eights guru, do you have a list?"

"You mean my completely un-superficial list of meaningful, soul-connecting qualities I'd like in a mate."

He traced his finger down her arm. "Yeah, that list."

She released a dramatic sigh. "I'm sorry to say that item number one is to find someone who's terrified of baby farm animals, so that disqualifies you right off the bat."

He shook his head. "I'm only *not* afraid of baby goats, thanks to you, so I think I get a pass on that one."

She raised her legs and stared up at the ruby-red heels. "Fine. You get a pass, but my soul mate can't expect me to wear these very often." She slipped off the sexy shoes, then gasped. "Oh no! My Birkenstocks and my cardigan!"

Shit! In the commotion of making sure she didn't break her leg or get mauled by a herd of drunk Brice Caseys, they'd left the items at the bar.

"We could call McGuires and see if they're still there," he offered.

She sighed. "No, I made a shoe trade with that girl, and if I'm being honest, that cardigan had seen better days. I think I just wore it to upset my mother."

He picked up one of the heels. "I'm not going to lie. You looked hot as hell strutting down that catwalk, but you're so much more than just a beautiful woman. You're smart and kind, and I really need to thank you for what you did for my dad," he finished, setting the heel aside.

"I think Michael Bolton was the real hero tonight," she teased.

"Georgie..." he began, but she cut him off.

"You beared witness to Lorraine Vanderdinkle and saved me from breaking my leg while participating in a wet T-shirt contest. I told you earlier, Jordan, we're even."

And then he remembered, and he reached for his phone. "Actually, you're way ahead."

She pursed her lips. "What do you mean?"

"Barry posted some footage and linked it to your blog page."

Georgie covered her face with her hands. "Is it awful?" she asked through her fingers.

The truth was, he didn't know.

"I didn't watch it yet. I just checked the score. We're only sixty likes behind the Dannies."

She dropped her hands. "Let's rip the bandage off. Do it. Push play."

"Are you sure?"

"Yeah, I need to see it, so I can start on damage control."

He took her hand into his. "Whatever it is, we'll figure it out together. We're a team."

She tightened her grip. "Okay, I'm ready."

He pressed play, expecting to see Georgie, but instead saw himself glaring at that loser, Brice Casey.

"If it takes a wet T-shirt contest for you to see Georgiana's beauty, then you never deserved her!"

And there it was, preserved for all to see, the moment where he took the beer and dumped it on Brice Casey's head. From there, the video switched to Georgie, strutting down the catwalk like she owned it until that bottle derailed her, and he was there to catch her.

He scrolled through her page. "The comments are really positive. Everyone seems cool with you entering the wet T-shirt contest and owning your femininity. They also seem to like getting a peek at your wild side," he answered as he continued to scroll through her page, then stopped, unable to hold back a grin. "And they like us together. There's a whole thread on what people think our kids would look like. Isn't that crazy," he added, now, wondering himself.

Georgie turned to him with a stunned expression. "Brice Casey was the catalyst for me starting the Own the Eights blog. I thought he really liked me *for me*, but he didn't. He said people expected a certain caliber of woman as his girlfriend. He wanted a ten and told me I was an eight at best."

Holy hell! Now, he was really glad he'd given the guy a Heineken bath.

Georgie narrowed her gaze. "How'd you know he was the guy who hurt me?"

"When you're not referring to me as the Emperor of Asshattery, you're calling me a Brice Casey. I put two and two together tonight when he introduced himself. Then, when you were working the runway, he came up to me and told me he thought you were hot—like you were just some object to him—and I hated him because he didn't see all of you."

Georgie glanced away. "What do you see when you look at me?"

He smoothed a lock of her hair back into place, knowing what he had to say. Done denying what his heart knew for sure.

"I see kindness, intelligence, and determination. I see you, Georgiana. I see all of you. And I want every part. I want you, and I want an *us*, a real us that goes beyond whatever happens with the contest."

She turned to him. "You do?"

"I do."

Georgie was the first woman, besides his mother, to set foot in his childhood bedroom, and he wanted her to be the last. But could it work? They stared at each other as if contemplating the next move in a game of chess, and she read his mind.

"Do you think an eight and a ten can make it?" she asked just as he remembered one salient data point.

"We do have a sixty-nine percent overlap," he replied, holding back a grin.

Her lips twisted into a sexy smirk. "So, we'll be fine as long as we're *sixty-nining*? Is that what you're trying to say?"

He was sure as hell ready to sixty-nine her into oblivion, but he wanted more. He wanted her.

He pulled her into his arms and leaned his forehead against hers. "As long as we're together, nothing can stop us."

"I agree," she whispered, her breath tickling his chin.

He wanted to take her, right there, but then he remembered who was waiting at home for her.

"Do you need to get home to take care of Mr. Tuesday?"

She chuckled. "You got his name right."

"Of course, I know his name. Do you think he's okay? It's been several hours."

She ran her fingertips down his jawline. "I texted Irene while you were with your dad. She brought Mr. Tuesday over to her place. I figured with how late it was, we might crash here."

"Always planning. That's a ten quality," he teased.

"Always conscientious. That's an eight for you," she countered.

But he was done caring about numbers, except for maybe sixty-nine.

"Can I kiss you, Georgiana? I don't think I've ever wanted anything more in my entire life."

A mischievous glint sparked in her eyes. "You can kiss me if you meet my Own the Eights list."

He raised an eyebrow. "So you're going to tell me?"

She nodded

"All right, I agree to those terms."

"Number one. He must be kind to animals and like Mr. Tuesday," she began.

He cupped her cheek and pressed his lips to hers in a slow, sensual kiss. "You know how I feel about goats, and I did save your dog from becoming a runaway and living on the streets."

She giggled. "Okay, number two. Must read books."

He nipped at her bottom lip. "I read books and journals and pertinent medical data."

"Oh wow!" she gasped and tangled her fingers into the hair at the nape of his neck, getting a little sidetracked.

"Keep going. Tens always finish what they start," he growled.

She let out a breathy moan as he gripped her ass.

"Numbers three, four, five, six, and seven. Do you have a stable job, are you always honest, do you donate to charity, care about the community, and want kids someday?"

"That's cheating," he replied.

"That's an eight being efficient," she shot back.

"Well, yes, yes, yes, yes, and yes," he answered, pressing a kiss between each response. He'd never even contemplated having kids, but with her, what had once seemed like roadblocks to his dreams, now felt very possible.

She rocked against him, and his cock sent the signal to wrap up this question and answer session.

He ran his tongue across the seam of her lips. "What's number eight, Georgiana?"

She trembled in his arms. "I always dreamed of being with someone who kissed me every night until I fell asleep."

His lips pressed to hers each night sounded like heaven.

"I can do that, but I should warn you now. There's not going to be much sleeping tonight," he said as their clothed bodies writhed together in the hottest, and first-ever, dry-humping session his bedroom had ever seen.

"I can live with seven out of eight," she answered with a sultry bend to her words that had his cock calling the shots.

He flipped her over and pressed her back into his bed as he pulled off his clothes then proceeded to remove her barely-there denim jean shorts and Superman T-shirt, revealing smooth, creamy skin and curves he'd never tire of worshipping.

He covered her body with his, his thick shaft settling between her parted thighs, and pressed a kiss below her earlobe.

He stilled. "Do we need a condom?"

She met his gaze. "I'm on the pill. As long as you're..."

"I am. I'm clean," he said a bit too quickly, sounding like an eager, horny teenager.

"Okay, number four on my list is honesty. And you did answer yes."

He held her gaze. "You can trust me, Georgiana. I'll never lie to you. Say you want this. Say you feel it, too."

They'd figure out the blog contest. They had to. There was no choice, not anymore. This hippie skirt-wearing, Birkenstock loving, cardigan donning bookseller beauty queen had peeled back the layers he'd constructed to shield his heart from his past. Yes, he was a ten now, and he still believed in the Marks Perfect Ten Mindset but with a slight tweak that dialed back the importance of image and appearance.

"I feel it, too," she said, then reached between them and gripped his cock. "Now, be a good ten and finish what you've started with this eight."

Jordan Marks did not need to be told twice. He drove inside her. Bare, with nothing between them, he paused. "You're the most amazing woman I've ever met."

She bit her lip. "I think you've lost the title of the Emperor of Asshattery."

"After tonight, I plan on earning a new title," he growled.

"Like a pageant?"

"Yeah, I'm going for the Emperor of *I made Georgiana come so many times she forgot her name.*"

"That would be tricky to get on a sash, but I'd enter that pageant," she said in a low, sexy rasp as he pulled back then thrust hard.

The time for pageant negotiations was over. And it was

damn time for this ten to get down to business when his eight surprised him.

"I want to be on top," she purred into his ear.

He maneuvered their bodies and gazed up at the goddess riding his cock. He gripped her ass as she pressed her hands against his chest, bucking and rocking, taking every inch of him into her sweet, hot center. He couldn't take his eyes off her. She was glorious, this beautiful, sensual woman who'd crashed into his life. He pressed his thumb to her tight bundle of nerves, and she arched her back, grinding into him. With a heated cry, she tightened around him, their bodies balancing on the precipice between desire and ecstasy when he thrust hard and sent them both spiraling over the edge.

They rode wave after wave of sweet, carnal release, gazes locked as if they needed this moment to solidify that they were together. But he didn't have to worry. Her sweet, sated smile told him this was no longer a stress relief screw. This was the real thing.

She collapsed onto him, and he wrapped her in his arms.

"You're not sleepy, are you?" he asked.

"No," she answered in a dreamy sigh.

He pressed a kiss to her temple, then lifted her from his chest and laid her next to him on the bed. He rolled onto his elbow and began dropping whisper-soft kisses to her lips.

"You look a little tired. We may need to work on your endurance," he teased, continuing his gentle assault.

"It's better than I imagined," she replied on another drowsy yawn.

"What is?"

"Falling asleep to kisses. An eight and a ten together. Oh, what will people think?" she said, nuzzling into him.

He pressed one last kiss to the corner of her mouth as her

breathing slowed, and she drifted off to sleep when a pang of anxiety shot through him.

Shit!

It wasn't people he was worried about. It was Deacon.

What would Deac say? Georgie was no Shelly. And thank God Georgie wasn't like that gym bunny. But Deac had his opinions. If he wanted to stay in the man's good graces, he needed to win. Dammit! He couldn't go there. He pushed the thought of Deacon's approval out of his mind, covered their bodies with a quilt folded on the end of the bed, and gathered Georgie into his arms.

But just as he was about to fall asleep, his gaze traveled to the dresser and the half-opened straw, and he could hear the kids chanting.

"Straws! Straws!"

He couldn't go back to what his life was like before he'd transformed into a disciplined ten.

Releasing a pained sigh, he shook off the memory and gazed at Georgie's beautiful, peaceful face. Could he have her and still be a ten?

He closed his eyes and focused on the sound of her breathing. He could do it. They could do it. There had to be a way where he could please both himself and his longtime mentor. A solution that allowed him to walk away with the girl and keep his relationship with Deacon intact.

Exhaustion washed over him, and on the cusp of sleep, all he could do was hope the answer would come.

11

GEORGIE

Georgie stared at her reflection in the dressing room mirror and frowned. "Jordan, I cannot have sex hair," she whispered as he stood behind her, kissing a sinfully sweet trail from her earlobe to her neck.

He met her gaze in the mirror and gave her a wolfish grin. "Like when it's all wild and tangled from us not leaving your place and *me* fucking *you* on every available flat surface in your bungalow?"

Well, he wasn't wrong.

It had been one hell of a Sunday...and Monday and Tuesday and Wednesday and half of a Thursday. She'd been rocking sex hair, camouflaged in a messier than usual bun, for the past few days, but she needed normal, un-sexed hair for at least the next couple of hours.

"But I like your sex hair," he said, back to focusing on her neck.

"Seriously, Jordan, when I was having my hair done, the stylist asked if I'd been camping or lived in a commune without running water."

He shrugged. "We've taken plenty of showers over the last few days."

She rolled her eyes. "Yeah! Sex showers that turned into sex out of the shower that brings us back to the sex hair which I do not have."

"For now," he teased, that sexy wolfish smirk still pulling at the corners of his mouth.

She leaned into him. It was no use trying to resist. This man turned her body to Jell-O—the good kind that wasn't prepared with enough grain alcohol to knock out a rhino. He ran his fingertips along her collarbone, and her skin tingled beneath his touch. She hummed a low sated moan, ready to give in to his advances, when a man's voice cut short their dressing room rendezvous.

"Mr. Marks, are you back here?"

Georgie's eyes popped open. "What will they think we're doing in here?" she whispered to the mirror version of Jordan Marks.

"I'm pretty sure the guys will be high fiving me. You look good enough to eat," he answered, pressing another kiss to her neck. And there was plenty of neck and shoulders to kiss in the strapless metallic silver gown, hugging her curves in all the right places.

CityBeat had tasked a group of personal shoppers, makeup artists, and hairstylists to fancy them up, for what, she didn't have a clue.

Earlier in the day, when they'd decided to try a particularly naughty sexual position from her research-purpose-only *Kama Sutra* book, their phones pinged with a CityBeat challenge address just as they'd experienced orgasm number six thousand four hundred twenty-two.

At least, that's what it felt like.

Her sex-hair twisted into a bun that would make even a

messy bun cringe, they followed the car's navigation app and had driven into a swanky part of town with boutique clothing stores and high-end salons. And over the course of the last few hours, she'd been waxed, buffed, polished, coiffed, and now shined like a new penny with an *un-sexed* updo.

She gazed at her reflection and had to agree. She looked pretty damn good.

After years parading on the pageant circuit, she'd shunned the primping part of being a woman. But with Jordan by her side, getting the male equivalent of their spa day, it was fun. There were no judges to impress and no scowling fake-eyelashed stage moms sizing each other up. The best part—it wasn't about her appearance. Jordan liked her for who she was, not what she looked like. His hungry, carnal gaze devoured her both dolled up in a ball gown and while rocking sweatpants and crazy bedhead.

With his knowledge of poetry and British literature and his magical tongue, her trifecta was totally pulling for this ten, who underneath it all, was an eight. But she'd decided she'd let him go on thinking he was a ten. He sure as hell had the abs for it, not that she was looking. Okay, she was. The man was built like a brick house and had the stamina of a suburban housewife camped out in front of a Wal-Mart on Black Friday.

He could go all night—and then some.

The man cleared his throat. "Sir, your tux just arrived. I'd like to check the fit."

"I'll be right out," Jordan answered, then dropped one last kiss to her shoulder.

She shooed him toward the door. "You better go. I don't know what they have in store for us, but I can't wait to see you in a tux."

"A little shallow for an eight," he teased.

She feigned exasperation. "A terrible habit I picked up from a ten."

He glanced down at his feet. "I really don't want to take these off, but I don't think they'll go with the penguin suit."

She held back a chuckle as she watched Jordan admire his Birkenstock-clad feet. "I told you they were comfortable."

Somewhere in their sex haze, they'd left her place to pick up some Chinese food and popped in the shoe store next door to the takeout place. Twenty minutes later, she'd gotten him to try on a pair, and her Nike-wearing ten experienced a Birkenstock baptism and became an immediate convert.

He took a step back, and his expression softened. "You look beautiful, Georgiana."

His low, gravelly voice sent the butterflies in her belly into flight.

She felt beautiful. He made her feel beautiful.

She held his gaze. "I'll see you in a little bit. Try not to make any of the ladies faint when they see you in that tux."

"There's only one person whose opinion matters," he said with a wink as he slipped out of the fitting room.

Her trifecta swooned, and Jane Eyre was back, handing out the fans.

But it wasn't just these sweet private moments that won over her fictional trio. To the delight of Mrs. Gilbert and her octogenarian clan of Michael Bolton fans and with Gene chuckling in the corner, Jordan had taken part in their weekly needlework time in the shop, not by crocheting but by removing his shirt and running back and forth in front of the shop's window, for ninety minutes straight, until Mrs. Rothchild's pacemaker went haywire.

His track pants riding low and his torso gleaming like a Greek god, she may have caught Jordan's eye a time or twenty as he passed by the shop.

And then, because she owed him big-time, she'd agreed to join him for a couple of training sessions at Deacon CrossFit. It turns out, it wasn't the roid-charged operation she'd envisioned. Instead, she found herself getting hot, not from push-ups, but from watching her ten in his element. And while he did take on a slightly cockier persona, which was pretty sexy, even Hermione agreed, it was as clear as day to see that his goal was to help his clients become a better version of themselves.

Deacon, however, was another story.

While the man was polite, she'd felt his gaze boring into her back anytime she'd interacted with Jordan. She got a weird quasi-jealousy vibe that didn't make much sense. Then again, maybe he thought she was just nuts when he'd asked her to pass him a kettlebell, and she'd searched the place for an actual tea kettle.

FYI: actual tea kettles are not a part of the CrossFit repertoire, which is really a shame, but also very good to know.

Georgie brushed all thoughts of Jordan's mentor aside and stared at her reflection as a pink blush colored her cheeks. She couldn't help it. That's what happened when all you could think about is the next time the guy you never expected to fall for lifts you into his arms as if you were as light as a feather then fucks you against the wall like you were the dirtiest girl on the block.

It almost didn't seem possible that she'd only met the former Emperor of Asshattery ten days ago.

Ten.

She couldn't really hate the number anymore. But it wasn't like she'd abandoned her Own the Eights principles. She'd just come to realize that chemistry mattered, but so did trust, honesty, mutual respect, and kissing. Lots of kissing.

A knock at the dressing room door cut through her daydream.

"Miss Jensen, your car's here."

Georgie ran her hands down the bodice of the dress and released a shaky breath when a young woman cracked open the door.

It was...Holy Miss Honey from the grocery store challenge.

"You don't know me. My name is Layla," the perky redhead honey enthusiast began. "But I know who you are. Of course, everyone here does."

"Do you work here?" Georgie asked, trying really hard not to look completely thrown for a loop.

The woman nodded. "I just wanted to tell you, I'd met Jordan before, at the market."

Oh shit!

"Oh yeah?" she answered instead, sounding a lot like she'd swallowed her tongue.

Layla looked away. "We kind of exchanged numbers, but I knew he wasn't going to call me."

"Oh, I..." Georgie replied, not sure how to respond to the woman's admission.

The redhead put up her hand. "Don't worry! I'm not telling you this because I'm some crazy woman who's been stalking him."

That was a damn crazy thing to throw out, but Georgie plastered on her beauty queen smile and let the woman continue.

"I decided to see if I could find him before I left the store, and I did. He was watching you so intently. I couldn't even be mad. I just hoped that someday, I could find someone who looked at me the same way he was looking at you."

Georgie's beauty queen expression made way for a genuine smile. "I'm sure you will. Have you checked out my Own the Eights blog? You may find some helpful tips on meeting your soul mate."

Layla's eyes lit up, and she started prattling on about how

everyone at the boutique was following the contest when a realization hit Georgie straight in the gut.

In a roundabout way, her blog had led her to Jordan.

"Is she coming?" a man called, cutting off the redhead's chatter.

One of the male stylists poked his head in the dressing room. "Mr. Marks is waiting for you, Miss Jensen."

"You better go!" Layla said excitedly, stepping out of the way.

"Thanks, and don't forget to check out Own the Eights!" Georgie said, picking up a metallic matching clutch.

She exited the dressing area to find everyone who'd helped them prepare for the evening, standing in a line. It was like a freaking episode of *Downton Abbey*. She channeled Lizzie Bennet—or at least what she'd thought Lizzie would be like after she'd become Mrs. Darcy and the lady of the Pemberley Estate—and thanked everyone graciously as she made her way to the door when Jordan appeared, and her heart skipped a beat.

Jordan Marks in gym attire was crazy attractive. Jordan Marks in jeans and Birkenstocks was super yummy. But Jordan Marks in a tux was a showstopper.

"Good luck!" Layla called, and Jordan's eyes went wide.

"That's..." he began.

"Yep, but don't worry. She's either really cool or totally stalking you. I'm not sure which," Georgie supplied, biting back a grin.

With a stunned expression, he waved goodbye to the redhead, then opened the car door and helped her inside the sleek black SUV.

Once the car started moving, he took her hand. "What do you think we're walking into tonight?"

Georgie shrugged then glanced down at her dress. "Probably not zip lining or scuba diving."

"Jesus, you kill me." He chuckled and pressed a kiss to her palm.

The SUV didn't have far to go. In a matter of minutes, the car pulled up to one of Denver's grand historic hotels, and a valet opened the door and helped her out.

"Welcome! The gala is being held in the main ballroom," the man said with a quick nod before moving on to the car pulling up behind them.

"It's a gala," she said to Jordan as he pressed his hand to the small of her back and led her inside.

"An after-school literacy program fundraiser. It sounds right up your alley," he added, gesturing to a banner in the hotel's lavish lobby.

"I know about them. I've donated books to this organization," she replied.

They entered the grand ballroom, packed with elegantly dressed women and men looking smart in their tuxedos when Barry emerged from a group of people and hurried over.

"You guys look great. Are you ready for tonight?"

She'd almost forgotten. CityBeat's founders, Hector and Bobby, loved a good twist. Anything could happen tonight, and there were plenty of CityBeat people filming and photographing the event.

She shared a look with Jordan. "We're up for anything. Have Daniel and Danielle arrived?"

The Dannies had more likes than them, but the brother and sister duo hadn't posted in a few days, which was odd. They usually produced so much content that it seemed like they'd need a team of people to do all the work.

Barry frowned. "They told us that a family issue had come up and that they couldn't make it tonight."

She and Jordan shared another look. He'd never been a fan

of the Dannies, but she couldn't help but hope they were all right.

"I just got off the phone with Danielle, and she assured me that she and her brother will be at the final event this weekend. But there have been some anomalies with their blog," the man added.

"What kind of anomalies?" Jordan asked.

"Nothing to worry about. Just odd surges with their follow-ers. I probably shouldn't have even mentioned it," the man said as beads of perspiration formed above his lip.

As it stood, the Dannies were in first place with her in second and Jordan a close third. It turns out, CityBeat followers love a good girl gone bad, and her wet T-shirt stunt had garnered the Own the Eights blog an avalanche of likes and new followers.

"Mentioned what?"

Georgie turned to find the CityBeat founders heading their way. The flamboyant Hector had gone with an electric blue tuxedo while the reserved Bobby stuck with the traditional black and white.

"Just talking about the contest, boss," Barry said, clearly nervous he'd dropped that little nugget of info.

"Well, one thing is for sure. People are loving our naughty bookseller," Hector said, greeting her with a kiss to the cheek.

Bobby adjusted his glasses. "And Jordan's goat breakthrough also set the platform on fire."

"Between you and me," Hector said, lowering his voice and putting a hand on Jordan's shoulder. "Goats always kind of creeped me out, too. Your phobia admission was quite inspiring."

Jordan blushed then cleared his throat. "I'm just happy that I helped some people address their fears."

"You two have quite a following now," Bobby said, glancing

at his phone, set to the Battle of the Blogs scoreboard. "And still with a sixty-nine percent crossover. It's amazing that no matter the increase in your followers, that number remains the same."

At the thought of sixty-nine, something they'd totally done thanks to the continuing *Kama Sutra* research endeavor, it was Georgie's turn to blush.

And the CityBeat community seemed to have taken notice of the chemistry between the eight and the ten. Despite thousands of blog comments asking if she and Jordan were a couple, they hadn't made anything official. Sure, the world watched as she got him through goat yoga and then when he'd defended her honor and dumped a beer on a guy's head before saving her from a nasty fall. But they were still competitors. A fact even the best sex and the sweetest gestures couldn't keep from the back of her mind. And while she desperately needed the prize money, she couldn't deny that Jordan's dream was any less worthy than hers.

"Jordan!" came a man's boisterous voice.

Jordan looked over his shoulder. "Deacon's here! Do you mind if I go say hello?"

"Not if you don't mind us stealing Georgie for a bit," Hector said, sharing a furtive look with Bobby.

She smiled up at Jordan. "I'll be fine. Tell Deacon hi for me."

He leaned in to kiss her, then glanced at his mentor and froze. "I'll only be a minute."

She nodded and tried to ignore the twist in her gut. Of course, he couldn't kiss her in the middle of a gala with the City-Beat founders standing two feet away. She had to be patient. The contest would end, and then they could figure out what to do next.

"Shall we," Hector said, gesturing to a table, and she was grateful for the distraction.

Barry bid them goodbye and headed back to the group of

CityBeat producers while she took a seat with Bobby and Hector, planting themselves one on each side of her.

"Looks like the eight and the ten may be a thing," Hector said with a coy smile.

"Um...well...you see...Jordan and I..." she began, sounding like a bumbling idiot.

"Opposites do attract," Bobby said, meeting Hector's gaze.

Hector chuckled. "They sure do. You thought I was a real jackass when we first met."

"How did you two meet?" Georgie asked, happy to shift the conversation away from her and Jordan.

Bobby adjusted his glasses. "Hector and I were assigned to work together on a project when we were seniors in college, and I was sure he was going to ruin everything."

"Until you fell in love with me and acknowledged my stunning intelligence," Hector added with a twinkle in his eyes.

Bobby smiled lovingly at his partner. "You see, Georgie, that project was the basis for the CityBeat platform. Hector and his crazy ways forced me out of my comfort zone. He made me see things differently."

Hector relaxed into the chair. "And Bobby did the same for me. On the surface, he was a quiet computer nerd, and I was a loud-mouthed know it all. It took us coming together to build something as brilliant as CityBeat and to learn that we weren't so different after all."

"That's such a sweet story," she said, glancing between the men.

"You and Jordan were certainly on opposite ends of the spectrum when we threw you two together. But it looks like things have improved," Hector said with his coy expression back in place.

"Oh...that," she replied, back to stammering like a guilty witness on the stand.

Bobby and Hector shared another knowing glance as the lights in the ballroom dimmed, and a man appeared on the stage at the front of the room.

"Oh, goody! It's time!" Hector crooned.

"Time for what?" Georgie asked.

Bobby leaned in. "Hector and I have a little wager going on for what might happen in the next four minutes."

Sweet *Pride and Prejudice*! A CityBeat twist!

"What's about to happen?" she asked when a spotlight illuminated their table.

"Ladies and gentlemen, thank you for coming out to raise money for our after-school literacy program, and thank you to CityBeat for kindly hosting the gala. Let's start our live auction with item number one, a private book club session with local bookseller and CityBeat Battle of the Blogs competitor, Georgiana Jensen."

She turned to Hector. "You put me up for auction?"

"It's nothing untoward. Whoever wins gets to have a book discussion with you. It's harmless and it's for charity."

"Oh boy," she said in a tight breath.

"Don't be shy, Georgiana. Join me up on stage," the man with the mic said, beckoning her to come forward.

Georgie stood, and like an undercover operative in enemy territory, she fell back on her training—her pageant training. Lifting her chin, she glided through the ballroom and onto the stage, rocking her gown and stilettos like she was born for the runway.

Take that Little Miss Cherry Pie!

"All right, folks. Who wants to spend an evening with this lovely lady talking books? Let's start the bidding at five hundred dollars."

Five hundred dollars!

Georgie scanned the ballroom for Jordan. Thank goodness

her ten stood out in a crowd. She found him quickly and caught his gaze.

"What's going on?" he mouthed.

She produced her beauty queen smile and gave him a slight shake of the head. She had no damn idea what was going on.

"Five hundred, right here!"

Georgie's head whipped to the side, and she squinted through the bright lights then gasped. "Save the Whales Steve? Is that you?"

"Hey, Georgie!" he called with a wide grin.

What the heck was he doing here? It did make sense that someone who cared about the whales would also care about youth literacy. He was an eight. But before she could give it any more thought, Jordan's voice rang out through the ballroom.

"Six hundred!"

Georgie's head whipped back to her ten, who'd lost the shocked expression. Now, determination burned in his gaze.

"Six hundred to the gentleman," the auctioneer called.

"Six fifty," Save the Whales Steve countered.

"Seven," Jordan shot back.

Seven hundred dollars to discuss the salient points of Jane Eyre. This was insane!

"Eight hundred," Steve bid, upping the ante.

"We have eight hundred dollars! Do I hear eight fifty."

You could hear a pin drop as everyone in the room watched the showdown.

"One thousand dollars," Jordan answered with a hard edge to his voice.

Her ten was not screwing around.

Save the Whales Steve took a step back and shook his head.

"All right! One thousand going once."

She held Jordan's gaze. She was sure he had the money, but he was saving for his dream.

"One thousand going twice."

His cool demeanor cracked, and he smiled up at her with such tender devotion that all she wanted to do was wrap her arms around this man and never let go.

"Sold to the gentleman for one thousand dollars."

She held his gaze until Deacon came up and tapped him on the shoulder. Jordan frowned as the man whispered something into his ear, then followed his mentor out of the ballroom.

The auctioneer led her off the stage, and she lost sight of Jordan and Deacon in the commotion. But one thing was for sure, she could tell from Jordan's strained expression that whatever Deacon had said, her ten wasn't pleased.

She headed toward the exit to catch up to them when Save the Whales Steve blocked her path.

"It's so great to see you, Georgie!"

She needed to get to Jordan. The tightness in her chest and the anxious flutter in her belly were not good signs, but that didn't give her license to be rude.

"Yes, it is," she answered, remembering her manners.

A man came up and wrapped his arm around Steve's waist. "Is this her?"

"Who's this?" she asked.

"Sorry, this is my boyfriend, Carson. I told him all about meeting you in the grocery store. When I saw you up on stage, I couldn't believe it was the cucumber girl. I told him, 'We have to bid on her!'"

The cucumber girl?

Well, there had to be worse nicknames, and she couldn't help but chuckle. Save the Whales Steve had had zero interest in her romantically. Jordan was going to get a real kick out of that.

"That was very kind of you to bid on me. But would you excuse me a moment? I need to find someone."

The men wished her well, and she set off, leaving the ballroom and was about to look for Jordan in the lobby when raised voices, Deacon and Jordan's voices, coming from an empty hallway caught her attention. Slowly, she made her way toward the sound then stopped next to the entrance to the ladies' room just out of the men's view.

"She's got you off track, Jordan! For fuck's sake, you wore Birkenstocks to the gym the other day."

"It's not like that, Deac. I know what my priorities are."

Georgie pressed her hand to her lips, holding back a gasp, hardly able to believe they were arguing about her.

Deacon threw up his hands. "Do you remember your priorities? Are you going to tell me right here, right now that nothing serious is going on with that girl? Because I can tell you one thing. She is not going to help you get ahead. And know this, I do not surround myself with losers. I hope you understand what I'm telling you."

She held her breath and waited for Jordan to respond.

"It's nothing serious, Deac. You know I'm in it to win."

She swallowed past the lump in her throat. Had she misunderstood? Had Jordan misspoken?

Deacon's callous smirk confirmed she'd heard him crystal clear.

Jordan's longtime mentor patted his shoulder. "Attaboy! Don't you ever forget that I took you under my wing. I made a warrior out of a weakling. Everyone knows you're my protégé, Jordan. Weakness from you would reflect poorly on me and the gym. I know you want to branch out on your own. I'm sure you can understand, I can only support you in that endeavor if I believe that you're one hundred percent committed to your goals. I need you to tell me because I think you may have forgotten. What's priority number one?"

A muscle twitched in Jordan's jaw as he looked away and mumbled something under his breath.

"Speak up, son!" Deacon barked.

Jordan met the man's gaze. "Win. Priority number one is to always win."

"Damn right. Finish what you start and crush *anyone* who gets in your way."

Georgie's heartbeat hammered in her chest, and the hallway went topsy-turvy just as the door to the women's restroom swung open, and she let out a surprised yelp.

"Oh, sorry! I didn't see you there!" a perky young woman she remembered meeting at Deacon CrossFit said, before glancing down the hall and spotting the men. "Deac, I'm not wearing underwear." The young woman giggled.

The men turned at the sound, and Jordan caught her gaze as his tanned skin went ghost white.

Deacon threw her an arrogant glance as the bubbly blonde hooked her arm with his.

"Isn't this so fancy, Jordan?" the woman said with another giggle.

"Good talk, son," Deacon said, eyeing Jordan one last time before escorting his date back toward the ballroom.

"Georgie," Jordan said, taking several steps forward, but she put up her hands defensively.

She steadied herself. "You lied to me. I thought that I was the one you were talking about when you said only one person's opinion mattered."

With his shoulders slumped, he shook his head. "I'm sorry, but it's complicated with Deacon. I owe him everything. He's been my mentor for over a decade, and he could make things very difficult for me in the CrossFit community."

How could he not see it?

She barked out a laugh. "That's not a mentor. That's a monster. A mentor supports you. What I just overheard might as well have been blackmail."

"That's just how Deacon talks," he murmured.

She shook her head. "No, that's how a mob boss talks. Do you actually want to be like that man?"

Jordan lifted his chin. "In some respects, yes. He put his own blood, sweat, and tears into making Deacon CrossFit the most profitable fitness chain in the state. And when I was nothing, he taught me how to be the best."

Anger surged through her veins. "Don't you see? You were never nothing! Skinny or ripped, that doesn't define who you are."

He glanced away. "It does to me."

Those four words cut like a dagger to her heart.

"Then you really are a ten, Jordan Marks," she shot back.

He met her gaze full-on. "Whatever made you think I wasn't, Georgiana?"

She stared into his cold eyes and bristled at his stony exterior. Who the hell was this? It certainly wasn't the man who'd just bid a grand on her. And it most definitely wasn't the man who'd made love to her and kissed her every night until she fell asleep in his arms.

A loud crash from behind caught her attention, and she whirled around to find Barry standing in the same spot she'd occupied when she'd overheard Jordan's conversation with Deacon.

The man opened and closed his mouth like a confused flounder. "Um, Georgie, Hector and Bobby wanted me to get your reaction to Jordan making the winning bid, but..."

But Jordan had reclaimed his title of the Emperor of Asshattery.

She glanced at the man she'd sworn she was falling in love with, then turned to Barry and schooled her features. "Here's a reaction. I'm leaving, and I never want to see Jordan Marks ever again."

"You haven't heard from him?"

Georgie set down a stack of books, then wiped the back of her hand across her forehead. "No, Becca, and that's the way I want it. I'm fine. I'm totally fine."

Her trifecta nodded. Yep, totally fine. Could not be finer. The finest of the fine.

Becca crossed her arms and leaned against the counter. "You've been carrying around that same stack of books and muttering to yourself all afternoon. I don't know if that constitutes as being fine?"

Georgie stared at the books. "I just want to find the right spot for them," she said as Mr. Tuesday came to her side and whimpered.

"You're even freaking out your dog," Becca added with a sympathetic grin.

Georgie scratched between her sweet pup's ears. Ironically, today marked eight days since she stormed out of the gala. Eight days since she'd had the taxi that she'd hailed to whisk her away stop at the market so she could buy the largest tube of vegan cookie dough they make. And eight days since she'd even glanced at her blog or anything online.

If somebody was owning the eights, it certainly wasn't her.

She glanced at her watch, then patted Mr. Tuesday's head. "I think it's time for our run, boy."

Mr. Tuesday perked up and scampered around her legs.

Becca pursed her lips. "Are you sure you want to do that 10K?"

Georgie blew out a weary breath. "Yes, I'm signed up, and it's the last official CityBeat event. They can crown the Dannies or Jordan, and then I can be done with it all."

"But you're not that far—"

"No, no, no!" Georgie said, cutting off her friend. "I told you. I don't want to know anything about the score or the blogs. I just want it to be over."

"Whatever you say, boss," Becca replied with a mock salute.

Georgie switched out of her Birkenstocks and into her running shoes, then grabbed Mr. Tuesday's leash and carefully fastened it to his collar. She'd started running the day after the gala. Determination or bullheadedness, or maybe it was her stupid longing to have some little piece of Jordan, she'd decided she'd take the time before the race to train and improve her stamina. It wasn't pretty. A lovely elderly woman using a walker passed her on her run yesterday, but it didn't matter. She may be the slowest runner on the planet, but she'd finish that damn race on her own.

She pulled her hair into a ponytail and turned to her friend. "I'm going to try and run all six point two miles today. Are you good to hold down the fort for a little while?"

"A little while? Georgie, I went on a run with you two days ago. You run a twenty-two-minute mile."

Georgie frowned. "Is that bad?"

Becca shook her head. "Not if you're a turtle."

"Well, it's almost the end of June. I'll try to be back before Thanksgiving. How does that sound?" she asked, opening the door.

Becca chuckled. "I'll be sure to save you some turkey."

Georgie left her bookshop and inhaled the fresh air. It was a gorgeous Colorado day with the majestic mountains to the west and the Tennyson business district bustling with friends and families out perusing the shops and eateries. She and Mr. Tuesday, who had no qualms with her running speed, thank you very much, headed toward the park.

She'd never admit it to Becca or Irene, but she'd picked this time on purpose. She knew Jordan's schedule and made sure to take her runs when he was training a client at Deacon CrossFit. And she didn't dare run past the gym for two good reasons.

One, if she ran into Deacon, she might punch the arrogant asshat square in his meathead mouth. And two, as much as she'd like to say that she carried the same vitriol for Jordan, she didn't. In fact, instead of forgetting the sole resident of Asshattery, she missed him more each day.

And here's what really stung. She had no one to blame but herself for her broken heart. She'd abandoned her Own the Eights principles, and in the throes of the crazy Battle of the Blogs competition, she'd lost her bearings and allowed her attraction to Jordan to knock her off course.

But one thing still remained. Bills. Many, many past-due bills.

She pushed the thought aside and continued down the street when a car honked a few sharp beeps, then pulled up alongside her.

Jeez! She might be slow, but it wasn't like she was holding up traffic! She was on the sidewalk, for Pete's sake!

She glanced over just as the back seat's dark tinted window rolled down.

"Georgiana! Pumpkin!"

Not even Michael Bolton could save her from the judgmental eye of Lorraine Vanderdinkle.

"What is it, Mom?" she asked, trying to speed up.

Oh, who was she kidding? This was her maximum pace.

"I'd like to speak to my daughter. I've sent you several emails, pumpkin."

"I'm not doing emails right now."

"Isn't that all your generation does? Eyes glued to a smartphone," her mother replied.

"I'm taking a break."

"To take up power walking?"

"I'm running, Mom."

"Pumpkin, that's not running."

She glanced at the car. "I could sprint. There's a bakery not far from here, and we both know my legs can really move when they're headed toward a doughnut shop."

A chorus of honks broke out behind the town car and her mother shook her head.

"Mrs. Vanderdinkle, would you like me to pull over? We're holding up traffic," came the measured voice of her driver.

"Georgiana! Will you please stop power walking so we can have a civilized conversation? I don't appreciate having to holler out of a car window."

A stream of angry Denverites edged up the road behind her mother's car, and Georgie gestured to a cluster of benches on the periphery of the park. "Okay. Take the next right. We can sit over there and talk."

Why couldn't her mother just spend the summer in the Mediterranean or the Maldives or anywhere with a Chanel within a ten-mile radius?

"Well, isn't this nice," Lorraine said, spreading a Hermes scarf on the bench before taking a seat.

Georgie hooked Mr. Tuesday's leash to the arm of the bench, then glanced at her mother.

"What's going on, Mom?"

The socialite folded her hands in her lap. "You haven't posted in days. I was starting to get worried."

Georgie stared at the least computer literate human on the planet. "Are you talking about my blog? The blog you can't even remember the name of?"

Her mother sat back and dusted imaginary crumbs off her linen pants. "You know he'd be proud of you."

Jesus! She wasn't ready for that. Her parents had divorced when she was young, and she'd grown up knowing two very different lives. One of opulence and wealth with her mother after she'd remarried Howard and one of cozy simplicity when she'd spend the non-pageant weekends with her literature-loving mechanic father. The father, who, on one beautiful summer day, much like today, had pulled over to help a family having car trouble, only to be killed instantly by a distracted driver.

Georgie stared at a point beyond her mother's shoulder. "Why would you say that?"

Her mother's features softened. "The bookstore, pumpkin. You were always your father's daughter. I knew our pageant days were close to being over when I'd find you in the event center bathrooms, hiding in a stall with your nose in one of the books your father left you."

Georgie frowned. "What are you talking about? All his books were donated to the public library."

Her mother shook her head. "Not all of them."

"What do you mean?"

"Pumpkin, after your father died, I brought you that box of books he'd left you. After that, I could barely get you to practice your runway walk, let alone try and improve your poise. Even now, good gracious! Shoulders back, Georgiana. A lady doesn't have to sit like a troll."

Georgie sat back, completely stunned. "Hold on. That wrapped box of books, the one with *Jane Eyre, Pride and Prejudice,* and the *Harry Potter Series*. Those were from Dad?"

"I thought I told you," her mother replied, looking genuinely confused.

Georgie thought back to that awful day. "No, I figured...I don't know what I figured. I just thought that you'd got them from somewhere to try and cheer me up."

"You thought I'd try and cheer you up with books?" her mother asked with a coy smile. "Your father passed away a week before your birthday. Those books were his gift to you."

"Those books have become really important to me over the years," she said, envisioning her trifecta, her confidants. Sure, they weren't real, but they'd become a guiding force in her life. The voice of reason, always cheering her on.

Had her father known this? Had he hoped that the heroines in these novels would inspire her to be her own woman? Did some benevolent twist of fate send her those books, days after his death, at the exact moment she needed the steadying hand and the reassurance her father had always provided?

Her mother smiled. "I'm sure that would make your father very happy. You two shared so many common interests. I tried to find something for us with pageants, but well, you turned out to be a bigger fan of doughnuts and Dostoyevsky. Did I say that correctly?"

Georgie nodded. "Yeah, you pronounced it perfectly."

A gentle breeze picked up, and silence stretched between the women.

"You know, I did love your father very much when we were younger. I was completely crazy for him back in high school. He was everything in our tiny town—handsome and smart," her mom said with a faraway look in her eyes.

Her mother rarely discussed her father, and Georgie quickly decided to take this rare opening to ask a question she'd been mulling over for years.

"I never understood what happened between you two. It wasn't like you guys fought or were cruel to one another, at least, not in front of me," she said, watching her mother closely and saw her not as the socialite caricature she'd pegged her as, but a woman, as complex and as nuanced as any other.

They'd always talked *at* each other. Today, they were actually talking *to* each other.

Her mother sat back and folded her hands in her lap. "We were so young, and we didn't know ourselves, not yet. And then you came along. You were such a beautiful baby. We killed it in the baby pageants."

Georgie cocked her head to the side and bit back a smile.

"You don't remember, but we did," her mother said with a sly grin before her expression grew pensive. "Your father and I had a different view of what we wanted our lives to look like. He was content with his books and fixing cars, and I had always dreamed about traveling and living well. Sometimes, two people can love each other but still not be right for each other."

Love each other but still not be right for each other.

Her mother must have caught wind about the blowout at the gala.

Georgie fiddled with the hem of her running shorts. She hadn't gotten online, so she had no idea how much of the exchange Barry had caught on camera, except for the part when she'd turned to him and spouted out how she never wanted to see Jordan again. She'd spoken those harsh words straight into his camera.

Did the whole world know of her humiliation? She'd told

Becca and Irene she didn't want any information about the blog or the contest, but surely, they would have made her listen if she were the laughingstock of the internet.

She stared at the ground. "Is that why you're here? You want me to understand that Jordan and I are too different to ever be happy together?"

Her mother laughed her million-dollar tinkling trill. "No, I'm here because I think that you and Jordan Marks love each other."

Wait, what?

Georgie's jaw dropped. "Why would you say that? You met him once, and we hadn't told anyone about us."

A knowing look sparked in her mother's eyes. "The ladies in my Pilates class are following your blog contest. They showed me the video of your recent foray into aqua adventure pageants."

Georgie's brow knit together. *Aqua adventure pageants*? Then it hit her. "Oh sh—" she half cursed, but her mother raised a hand.

"No, profanity, pumpkin!"

Georgie could feel the hot blush creeping up her neck. "Mom, if I even thought for a second that you were reading my blog and would see that footage, I would have warned you."

"Warned me? Why would you have done that?" she asked.

Georgie cringed. "Because it was a wet T-shirt contest at a bar that got broadcast across the globe."

Her mother waved her off. "No, no! I was actually quite pleased to see you on the stage. Your foot placement was perfect. Your makeup was spot on. Minus the fact that your breasts were on display, your posture rivaled that of a Russian ballerina. I don't know if I've ever been prouder."

Georgie continued to scan the ground, searching for a sinkhole to swallow her up and save her from this conversation. But the earth didn't move. Thanks a lot, planet!

Georgie sighed. "What would make you think that Jordan and I love each other?"

Her mother's coy expression was back. "That wasn't the only video I watched. You helped that man hold a goat, and then he was there to catch you when you fell off that stage," she added.

Georgie shook her head. "None of that matters now."

"And then, there was the gala video," her mother said, pressing on in true Lorraine Vanderdinkle fashion. "Those two men bidding on you! It was thrilling. And the look on Jordan's face. Pumpkin, that man cares for you deeply."

Georgie tucked an errant lock of hair behind her ear. "I thought so, too. But I was wrong."

"Well, the whole CityBeat website is buzzing about the two of you. Neither of you have posted anything since that day. And the last video was a snippet of you saying you never wanted to see Jordan again. Everyone wants to know what happened."

What happened? Her world came crashing down around her in the space of two minutes. That's what happened.

She met her mother's gaze. "I overheard a conversation where Jordan had the chance to let someone very important to him know that he cared for me, and he failed." She shook her head. "No, not just failed. He sold me out. All the things he'd said, like how he cared for me and how he wanted to be with me, they were all lies. He only cares for himself."

Her mother leaned in. "You didn't see his face after you turned away from him."

"Mom, I don't want to know—"

"We're not always the best version of ourselves," her mother said, cutting her off. "I tried to make you into something you weren't. I dragged you to pageants all over the country. And for years, you indulged me when I should have been taking you to the library or wherever book people go. At the time, I did what I thought was best for us, but I wasn't thinking about us. I was thinking about myself, thinking about how I didn't want to end up like my mother, scrubbing floors and cleaning houses. I wanted you to have the life of a princess, and that clouded my ability to take into account what you wanted."

Looking at her mother, you'd never know that she'd come from nothing. And then she thought of Jordan and that drawer filled with straws.

"I'm proud of who you are, Georgiana," her mother continued, breaking into her thoughts.

Georgie shook her head. "You don't have to say that, Mom."

"Why not? I'm proud of the woman you've become. I read all your blog posts. And while I may beg to differ on your view of minimal makeup use because a woman always needs to have her lips and eyes accentuated. I did read all the comments. You've helped many people, pumpkin."

"Then you get it," she said, holding her mother's gaze.

Her mother nodded. "I understand that you value character."

"I do."

"And kindness."

"Yes."

"And integrity."

"Absolutely."

Her mother paused. "What about forgiveness? Could you forgive me for all the pageant years?"

This threw her for a loop. "Of course, Mom," she answered.

Her mother patted her hand. "Sometimes, we make the wrong choice. That doesn't always mean we care any less. Has he tried to contact you?"

Georgie swallowed past the lump in her throat. "I blocked his number and had my friend's husband, who is a client at the gym Jordan works at, deliver a message that I'd sic my dog on him if he tried to call me or come by the shop."

"That dog?" her mother asked with a skeptical bend to her words.

Mr. Tuesday had curled up on the grass. Always one for a snooze, he yawned in his sleep.

She scratched between the napping dog's ears. "He's normally more ferocious. But here's the thing, Mom, I made a promise to myself when I started the Own the Eights blog. I swore I wasn't going to fall for another good-looking jerk again."

Her mother chuckled. "Oh, Georgiana, I don't think you fell for Jordan because he's handsome."

Her mother was right. She hadn't.

Georgie glanced at the tree where she'd met Jordan and called him a supreme asshat after he'd caught her squirrel-chasing pooch.

"Even if Jordan did apologize. Even if he swore that I meant everything to him. I'm not sure what he could do to make me believe it," she answered, her gaze still locked on the tree.

"Mrs. Vanderdinkle."

Georgie startled, then glanced over her shoulder to see a man in a black suit.

"Yes, John. Oh, Georgie, this is John, our new driver."

The man nodded politely. "Mr. Vanderdinkle called to remind you of your doubles tennis match with the Lockwoods this afternoon."

"Thank you, John. I'll just be a moment," her mother answered, then turned to her. "I know you'll do what's right for you, pumpkin."

Georgie rubbed her fingertips to her temples. "I wish I knew what that was."

Lorraine Vanderdinkle stood and gathered her designer scarf from the bench. "You could start by getting back to your blog and possibly allowing Howard and I to buy you a Barnes and Noble. Those are bookstores, right?"

Her well-meaning socialite mother could really lighten a situation.

Georgie sighed. "I don't think you can buy just one."

"Would you like all of them?" her mother countered with a sly smirk.

Georgie chuckled, now understanding the kindness in her mother's insane proposal. "No, but it's really nice of you to offer."

Her mother folded the scarf into a tiny square. "The CityBeat site says that they'll be live-streaming the Denver Trot 10K tomorrow afternoon and that all the Battle of the Blog competitors will be there. Are you planning on power walking in it?"

"Yes, I'll be there *power walking*," she acquiesced as she normal-walked her mother over to the town car.

"So, you'll see him there."

Georgie shook her head. "Probably not. He's Mr. In-It-To-Win-It. I'm sure he'll fly by me and not even notice."

Her mother took her hand and gave it a gentle squeeze. "You never know, pumpkin. It's going to be live on the internet. Anything can happen."

13

Jordan entered Deacon CrossFit and stared at the empty receptionist's desk. The desk where Shelly's ass should be planted.

"Hey, Jordan! I didn't expect to see you today. Don't you have the Denver Trot 10K later on?"

He nodded to Sara, one of their best trainers, then glanced at his watch. "I've got a little over an hour until it starts, but I wanted to check on a few things. Why are you here?"

The gym was only open half-day on Saturdays for clients to make up missed sessions during the week and Sara hadn't missed any of hers.

The trainer looked away. "Deac asked if I could close today."

What the hell?

"Why can't Shelly close? I made the damn schedule and gave you the day off because I know your kids have soccer on Saturdays."

The woman shrugged. "I think Deacon has another *assignment* for Shelly."

He nodded as a muscle ticked in his jaw. He was in no mood for this bullshit. Shelly was the damn reason he had to come in, and she was the last person he wanted to see.

The past eight days had been pure hell. He'd tried to apologize, but Georgie had cut him off, and he couldn't blame her. So, he'd thrown himself into training and took on new clients by the dozen. And he'd stayed the hell away from the internet and the CityBeat site. Thank Christ, he hadn't gotten any challenge texts, but he had to show up for the race.

A central principle of the Marks Perfect Ten Mindset, always finish what you start—and crush it.

Still, he did owe Georgie an apology. He wasn't that big of a douchebag not to know that he'd hurt her. But even though Deacon's words at the gala were harsh, the man was right. He'd gotten off track. He'd lost focus. And there was no way he was going back to a life of failure. The life of Jordy "Straws" Marks.

His head understood that it had to be this way. Unfortunately, his heart felt like it had been run through a meat grinder.

"Go ahead and take off, Sara. I can close up."

"Thanks, Jordan. If I hurry, I can catch the end of the game," the woman said, with a grateful expression as she picked up her gym bag and hurried out the door.

Jordan scanned the empty gym then headed back to his office. Jesus! It was a real dick move to call in Sara. What was Deacon thinking? He turned the handle and opened the door and saw precisely what Deacon was not only thinking but doing.

Namely, Shelly.

"Christ, Deac!" he exclaimed, turning away from Shelly, bent over his desk, with Deacon nailing her from behind.

He slammed the door, anger prickling through his body, and waited for the office fuck fest to end.

It didn't take long. Barely a minute had passed before Shelly opened the door, fully dressed—thank God—and exited his office with a cotton-candy-brained giggle.

"Oops! Sorry, Jordan," she said, blond ponytail bobbing from side to side as she grabbed her purse and left through the front door.

His anger had gone from a low simmer to a full boil when Deacon called him into the office. He entered to find the man sitting on the edge of the same desk where he was screwing their receptionist.

"Twenty-two years old, and she likes to fuck in public places. Restrooms, elevators. She's waiting for me in the bathroom at that little bistro down the street so I can screw her brains out in one of the stalls. Do you know how much Viagra I have to take to keep up with her?" Deacon said, chuckling to himself as if he hadn't just broken a shit ton of employment laws.

Jordan schooled his features, swallowing his revulsion. "Yeah, Deac, we need to discuss Shelly. An error came up in the payroll. Somehow, her salary tripled."

His mentor crossed his arms. "It's not an error."

"She makes more than our best trainers," Jordan threw back.

A greedy little smirk pulled at the corners of Deacon's lips. "Well, none of those trainers can give a blow job like they were born to do it."

Jordan took a step back. "You gave Shelly a raise because she's good at giving head?"

Deacon narrowed his gaze. "She's twenty-two, Jordan. She's good at giving everything."

Jordan looked away as disgust washed over him. What the hell had happened to the man he'd looked up to? The man he'd idolized for a decade.

He lowered his voice. "We need to talk about her salary. You can't make a change like that and not tell me. I'm in charge of the books."

"And it's my goddamn gym, Jordan. *Deacon* CrossFit. When you get your ass in gear and start your own business, you can screw all the twenty-two-year-old receptionists you want. By the way, have you won that contest yet?"

The muscles in his chest tightened as contempt for his long-time mentor set in. But before he could answer, Deacon's phone pinged.

Jordan crossed his arms. "Is it Shelly? Is she ready to screw you in the toilet?"

Deacon's cocksure expression gave way to panic. "Shit! No, it's Maureen. She's got the girls with her. I forgot I had them today." The man set down his phone. "I need you to do me a favor, Jordan. Go up front and tell them I'm not here. Tell them... Shit! Tell them I'm on a long run with a client."

"You haven't trained anyone in years," Jordan threw back.

"Just get rid of them, and I'll add a little extra onto your salary, too," Deac pleaded, his words as slimy as a fucking snake.

"This is bullshit," he said, leaving the office just as Deacon's daughters bounded through the front door, followed by their mother.

"Jordan," the twin girls exclaimed.

They'd gotten so big. He'd started working with Deacon when they were just babies, back when his mentor worked hard at building his business and also at being a father and a husband.

When did everything change?

He smiled down at the girls. "Tell me if I get it right. You're Mia, and you're Mya," he said, purposefully mixing up their names, a little game they'd been playing for years.

The identical twins giggled.

"No! I'm Mya, and she's Mia," Mya said, wrapping her little arms around his waist.

"I'm sure I'll get it right someday," he said, happy to see the girls.

"Can we climb on the big tire?" Mia asked, bouncing from foot to foot.

Jordan glanced over his shoulder at the four-hundred-pound CrossFit tractor tire they used when training clients. "Sure! Just don't pick it up and throw it out the window."

The girls laughed and set off to play as he greeted Maureen with a kiss to the cheek.

"How are you?" he asked.

The woman, who had been like a second mother to him, cocked her head to the side. "I should be asking you the same thing, Mr. CityBeat Battle of the Blogs."

Heat rose to his cheeks. "You're following that?"

"Everyone I know is following the contest. You and the Own the Eights blogger are the hottest thing on the internet."

Georgie. Just the mention of her tightened the vice clamped around his heart.

"Yeah, that..." he answered, sure his cheeks had bloomed a bright shade of scarlet.

Maureen eyed him carefully. "You two are great together. But nobody can figure out why she's so angry with you."

He sighed. "It's me. I led her on and then had to end it with her because I forgot my priorities."

The woman frowned. "What are your priorities, Jordan?"

He was ready with his canned answer. "I'd like to start my own gym and run my own show."

"You want to be like Deacon?" she asked, concern etched on her face.

Jordan glanced at the girls, jumping in and out of the super-sized tire, then met Maureen's gaze. She'd supported her husband every step of the way. She'd done his books in the beginning. She'd cleaned the locker rooms and dusted the weights. She worked the front desk, even while nursing the girls.

And what had Deacon done? Thrown it all away to screw twenty-two-year-olds in an elevator.

He couldn't lie to this woman. And that's when it hit him. His mentor was a goddamn fool. He'd had it all—a kind, loving wife and two bright, healthy girls. And he couldn't see it. He hadn't factored them into his definition of success. Sure, Deac was wealthy and connected, but what was all that without love?

"No," he said in a tight whisper. "I don't want to be like Deacon. I really screwed up with Georgie. She's..."

"She's what, honey?" Maureen asked, her expression softening.

He blinked back tears. Jesus! He hadn't cried since he'd lost his mother.

He steadied himself. "She's everything. She's everything I never knew I needed and everything I don't want to live without."

How could he sell her out? This woman who'd shown him such compassion. This former Miss Cherry Pie who was always on his mind. This complex, beautiful, courageous, Birkenstock wearing, bun-sporting beauty he'd been sure was his polar opposite, an eight in his sea of tens, who'd completely changed his life.

Maureen glanced around the gym, taking in her ex-husband's only measure of success. "You don't get many second chances in this life, but you owe it to yourself to try. You'll see her today, right?"

That's right! The 10K! Thanks to Deacon's office sexcapades debacle, he'd almost forgotten.

He checked his watch. "Yeah, I will. But I need to get to her before the race. I have to talk to her."

"Is daddy here?" Mya chirped, breaking into their conversation.

"Yeah, Daddy had to cancel our visit last week, but he said he'd take us to the zoo today!" Mia added.

Jordan grabbed a sheet of Deacon CrossFit stationery and an envelope from the front desk and wrote the words he should have said to Deacon months ago.

I quit. Effective immediately.

He signed the brief note, folded the paper, then slid it into the envelope. He was done being Deacon Perry's righthand man, and he sure as hell wasn't about to lie to his children so he could go screw some college student in a bathroom.

He called the girls over. "I need to go do something important. Could you give this to your dad for me?"

Mia took the envelope. "He's here! Daddy's really here?"

"Yep, he's back in the office," Jordan answered.

Deacon was not going to be a deadbeat dad on his watch.

The girls skipped through the gym toward the back office, and he turned to Maureen.

"I can't continue to work for Deacon."

"I know," she answered.

"And I hate to run out like this, but I've got to try and get Georgie back."

Maureen squeezed his hand. "From the first time you set foot in the gym, all those years ago, I knew you were one of the good guys."

"Thanks, Maureen. That means a lot coming from you."

Her eyes shining, she gestured to the door. "Go win back your girl."

At a speed that would have rivaled that of The Flash, he tore out of the gym and sprinted down the street. Heading straight for Georgie's bookshop, an idea for a blog post sparked. He had to make his feelings known. He had to get his apology out there for all to see and let the world know that he loved—yes, loved— Georgiana Jensen.

When he'd wanted to be like Deacon, it wasn't the millionaire screwing twenty-somethings he admired. It was the entrepreneur who loved his wife and daughters. His mentor may have veered off the path, but he didn't have to sacrifice love for success. Building a life with Georgie would be all the success he'd ever need.

His pulse racing, he burst into the bookshop and caught a glimpse of a woman with a messy bun holding up a book. "Georgie! I don't care if you sic Mr. Tuesday on me, I need to talk to you. I love you. And I'm sorry. I'm so sorry."

The woman lowered the book.

The woman was not Georgie.

"Are you having a seizure?" Becca, Georgie's part-time employee, asked.

He shook his head. "I don't think so."

He did feel out of his mind but in a really good way.

Mr. Tuesday came out from behind the counter, and Jordan knelt down to greet the pup.

"Sic 'em, boy," Becca commanded.

The dog cocked his head to the side.

"Well, it was worth a shot. What do you want, Marks? We're fresh out of the new release of *How to Be a Douchebag*. But, you seem to already have gotten that down."

"Is Georgie here?" he asked, completely deserving of all the shit Georgie's friend could dish out.

Becca narrowed her gaze. "No, she left for the race. Why are you here?"

He threw up his hands. "Did you not hear the whole *I love Georgie and don't want to live without her* declaration?"

"Oh, I heard it. I also heard you threw her under the bus," Becca answered with an epic eye roll.

He took a step forward. "I screwed up. I know, and I'm going to fix it," he said, then glanced at the laptop on the counter. "Is that yours?"

"The laptop?"

"Yes."

"Yeah, it's mine."

He moved in closer. "Can I borrow it? I need to make a blog post."

Like a row of dominoes colliding in a long line of rapid motion, his thoughts came together, each imaginary click sparking a line of text. A manifesto. A love letter. An epiphany.

If people thought his goat revelation was touchy-feely, they hadn't seen anything yet.

"Why the hell should I let you use my laptop?" Becca asked.

"Because I love Georgie. I do. The Marks Perfect Ten Mindset is total bullshit and I need to let the world know," he answered, praying she'd see he wasn't kidding.

She drummed her fingers on the counter. "Do you know that you're all neck and neck? You, Georgie, and the Dannies are all within a few points of each other. Think about it. The money, the notoriety. If you played your cards right, it could be yours."

He had no idea the contest was so close. But he also knew that Becca was testing him, seeing if he'd jump at the opportunity to win. He wasn't about to fall for her trap. Nothing could change how he felt about Georgie, and he knew what he had to do.

He blew out a tight breath. "Then I really need to get this down. Can I please use your laptop? It'll take me forever to write this hunting and pecking on my phone."

Becca watched him for what seemed like a freaking eternity, then opened the laptop and turned it toward him. "This better be damn good."

"Thank you," he said, navigating to the CityBeat page.

He logged into his account and started typing.

Sixty-nine isn't just a sex position.

"Hold up, mister!" Becca called from over his shoulder, snooping in on his post.

"It's not what you think. Sixty-nine percent of my followers also follow Georgie. She'll know what it means."

"Are you also planning on doing the 10K today?" she asked.

He nodded. "Yes, I have to get to her."

Becca looked at her watch. "You better type, Marks. You're going to be cutting it close."

His fingers flying, he poured his heart into the post. His past. His drawer of straws. His mother's death. And how Georgie had made him a better man, and how he'd epically let her down. Nothing was off-limits. The world was about to learn that Jordan Marks wasn't always a ten.

He stared at the wall of text. His confession for all to read.

"That's really good, Jordan," Becca sniffed, still reading over his shoulder.

"Do you think so?"

She nodded, brushing a tear from her cheek. "You should post a link to this on all your social media sites."

"That's a great idea," he said, then checked his watch. "Shit!"

"What's wrong?"

"The race starts in seventeen minutes. Can you do it for me?"

Becca blew her nose. "Yeah, but I'll need your passwords."

"There's only one. It's Marks Ten as one word."

Becca's jaw dropped. "That's your password?"

"Yeah."

"That's a terrible password," she scoffed.

Dammit! She was right.

He shrugged his shoulders. "I should really change it."

"You think? Seriously, it's the worst. Like, on a scale of one to ten, your password is a two at best. Maybe a one. I'm surprised your ass hasn't been hacked yet."

"Message received. I will change the password, but first, I need your help getting this out there," he said, watching the second hand on his watch tick away time.

"Okay! Go! I've got it," Becca answered, shooing him away when his stomach emitted a piercing, mega-growl.

Shit! It had been hours since he'd eaten.

He looked around for a muffin or a doughnut. "I'm going to have to sprint to the race. Do you have anything here I can eat? I'll need some energy."

"All we have is this. Georgie's been living off the stuff since the gala," Becca said, opening the door to a mini-fridge below the register and taking out a tube of vegan cookie dough.

He smiled, remembering Georgie in that god-awful cardigan, tearing open the tube with her teeth and power eating the dough after their first challenge.

"Hey, Romeo! Snap out of it," Becca said and tossed him the tube. "You better be able to eat and run, buddy. The race starts in eight minutes."

Eight minutes.

If anyone ever needed to own the eights, it was him.

14

Georgie glanced around, raised her arms and stretched, mimicking the real runners packed in around her. This was it. The Denver Trot 10K, sponsored by CityBeat. With the CityBeat logo splashed on T-shirts and event banners and with a team of City-Beat producers walking through the crowd, snapping pics and taking videos, there was no doubt that today was a big day. Spectators lined the Denver streets, closed off to traffic for the race, and carried signs with pictures of her and Jordan and the Dannies.

Today, a winner would be chosen.

She'd wanted this, right? She'd dreamed of gaining new followers and increasing her visibility online. She'd wanted to take her Own the Eights blog and make it big, make it a force for good and help people find their true soul mate.

And now?

Now, all she wanted was for it to be over.

After eight days of ignoring her blog, she was sure she'd be in last place. She'd written off the prize money. She could tighten up her budget, sell her car, or try for another bank loan to make ends meet. Her trifecta got it. With their girl-power guidance, sent to her from her beloved father, she'd figure it out.

Hurdle number one was simply getting through today.

She glanced around, looking for Jordan, unable to help herself, when the Dannies, all perfect bone structure and matching running gear, made their way toward her.

"Well, look at you! Aren't you the little runner," Danielle said with a swish to her blond ponytail.

But Daniel looked far less enthusiastic.

"This is a stupid idea. We shouldn't be here," the Ken doll lookalike said, shifty-eyed and watching the crowd.

Danielle amped up her smile. "If we want to win the money, we have to be here."

Georgie glanced between the siblings. "Yeah, you guys have missed a couple of challenges."

Danielle huffed an exaggerated sigh. "It's so hard when everyone wants a piece of you. We have so many balls up in the air. So many people and companies wanting to work with us thanks to our skyrocketing blog numbers, right Daniel?" she added with a slight edge to her voice.

"Yeah, sure, whatever," he replied, pulling up his hoodie and continuing to scan the crowd like a paranoid mannequin.

Georgie raised an eyebrow. "Is he okay?"

A slight blush colored Danielle's porcelain cheeks. "He's just scoping out our competition. By the way, where's your team-mate? There's not any trouble in paradise, is there?" she asked with a little smirk.

This bitch! Hermione raised her wand to knock this Danny into next week, while Jane and Lizzie readied their teacups to hurl the hot liquid at the woman's smug face.

Daniel leaned in toward his sister. "I want to get this over with. Let's get to the front of the pack."

"May the best team win," Danielle said over her shoulder but with a lot less bite to her words as the Barbie-bot scanned the crowd.

Oh, screw them! And what did they have to be nervous about with their *skyrocketing numbers* and numerous entrepreneurial opportunities? Still, Daniel's level of unease was weird.

Georgie went back to her stretching when another voice called out to her, and she inwardly cringed. Maybe Daniel had the right idea by hiding under a hoodie.

"Hey, Georgie!" Barry said, weaving through the crowd. "Hector and Bobby wanted me to stick close to you during the race to get some footage."

Georgie held back a groan. As much as she wanted to tell Barry to get lost, he was only doing his job.

She tried to muster a smile. "No problem."

The man started to reply but stopped when his phone began buzzing and pinging like crazy. He stared at the screen, his eyes going wide. "You've gotta see this, Georgie."

Oh, hell no! If there was a day to stay off the internet, it was today.

She took a step back. "Nope, I don't want to see anything."

"Georgie, it's amazing. It's—"

"GO!" a voice bellowed over the massive speakers stacked around the starting line.

Music blared as the race participants scrambled to separate themselves from the pack. Georgie popped in her earbuds and settled into her running pace. Poor Barry wasn't going to get much of a performance out of her today. No baby farm animals and no wet T-shirt shenanigans. She'd zone out, finish the race, then stop by the shop and gorge on her last tube of vegan cookie dough.

The 10K was six point two miles, and Georgie gave a little sigh of relief when she passed the five-mile marker. So far, so good. She wouldn't have called her encounter with the Dannies fun, but it was painless, and she hadn't laid eyes on Jordan once. While she'd started the race in the back of the pack, he'd probably gotten there hours early with the tips of his toes grazing the starting line, ready to take off like a shot.

"Always win. Always finish what you start. Always be the best. I'm Jordan Marks, the perfect ten, and I always crush it," she murmured under her breath, doing her best Emperor of Asshattery impression.

"Is that what I sound like?"

Even with her earbuds in and Michael Bolton belting away —yes, she added the lyrical genius's music to her playlist—the delicious, treacherous shiver spreading through her body could only be in response to one person.

Willing herself not to trip or fall ass over elbow, she glanced at Jordan, walking alongside her and holding...

"That better not be my vegan cookie dough!" she exclaimed.

His eyes widened, and he looked like a kid who'd just gotten caught with his hand in the vegan cookie jar.

"You went to my shop and took my cookie dough?" she tried to yell, but it was damn hard to do while running.

"I was looking for you, and it's more complicated than that," he answered.

She had to look away because she couldn't take the depth of emotion in his eyes, and she sure as hell couldn't allow herself to feel an ounce of compassion. Not after how he'd treated her.

She doubled her resolve. "What do you mean, it's not that complicated? Is that my cookie dough?"

"Yes."

"You are so the reigning Emperor of Asshattery," she grumbled.

"And I thought you were going to run this race," he replied, gesturing with the opened tube of dough.

"I am running!" she barked.

"That's a power walk, Georgie."

"Gah!" she cried, then turned to the CityBeat producer on her other side. "This is running. I'm running, right, Barry?"

"Well..." the man answered with a nervous expression.

These stupid men!

"Georgie, I'm not here to critique your power walking," Jordan said, then shook his head as she threw daggers at him with her eyes.

"Running! I meant running. I'm not here to critique your *running*. I'm here because I love you."

Love?

Her trifecta swooned and clutched each other, but Georgie wasn't about to fall for this.

"You've got a really funny way of showing it. And stealing my last tube of cookie dough isn't doing you any favors."

"Georgie, please, let me explain," he said just as a voice rang out from the spectators lined up along the side of the road.

"Sixty-nine isn't just a sex position, Georgie!"

"Jordan loves you, Georgie!" another voice cried.

She stopped. The finish line was in sight, but she needed to know what the hell these people were yelling about.

"What's going on, Jordan? And why are people calling out sexual positions?"

"Because of sixty-nine, Georgiana," he answered, his voice cutting through the air and quieting the boisterous crowd.

Holy crazy man! Maybe Jordan had lost his mind. Maybe he'd done one too many of those teakettle lifty thingies and blew a gasket.

An eerie quiet set in as Barry continued recording and Jordan pulled out his phone.

"I wrote something for you. Will you just listen to me for a minute?"

She crossed her arms. "Make it fast. I have to finish this damn race and then stop at the grocery store for another tube of cookie dough."

Jordan released a shaky breath. "Okay, are you ready?"

She glanced around. No one moved a muscle. The other race participants were either staring at them or looking at their phones. Even the damn breeze stilled as if nature herself wanted to listen.

"Yes, I'm ready," she said, completely not ready.

Jordan swallowed hard. "Dear Georgiana, sixty-nine isn't just a sexual position. It's our overlap. It's the statistical proof that we were never polar opposites. I may have started out in this competition as a ten. I may have preached the benefits of the Marks Perfect Ten Mindset to anyone who'd listen. But what's the point of being a ten when the woman I love wants an eight?"

Emotion flooded her chest. "Why are you saying this?"

He held her gaze. "Because I mean it. I was a colossal idiot. I lost track of what was really important. I screwed up my priorities."

She willed her bottom lip not to tremble. "I know. I heard you agree with Deacon when he said I was a distraction."

Jordan shook his head. "No, you were never a distraction. I was off track. But it wasn't because of you. You, Georgiana, you are my priority. And you were right. Deacon didn't have my best interests at heart. But you know who did?"

She broke their connection and stared at the ground. If she looked at him, she might just fall apart. In her heart of hearts, she wanted it to be true. But how could she trust him? How could she know he wouldn't hurt her again? She was about to tell him they could never make it work when her mother's words, of all people, popped into her head.

Sometimes, we make the wrong choice. That doesn't always mean we care any less.

She met his earnest expression with a skeptical eye. "How can I trust you? How can I know that you mean what you're saying?"

He handed Barry the tube of vegan cookie dough, then reached out and held her hands.

She couldn't help lacing her fingers with his. But these weren't the strong, steady hands that had held her close.

"You're shaking, Jordan."

"It's because I'm terrified," he replied, his eyes shining.

"Of losing the contest?" She had to ask.

"No, of losing you."

She wanted to take that step forward, close the distance between them, and let him wrap his arms around her, but she couldn't. Not yet.

"Those are just words."

Jordan nodded, then glanced toward the finish line. "One of the Marks Perfect Ten Mindset tenets is to always finish, right?"

She knew this song and dance.

She sighed. "Yes, along with a bunch of other hyper-masculine motivational bullshit."

He chuckled as his gaze grew glassy. "How about this? How about we *don't* finish this race together. Let's turn around, start walking, and never look back."

"What about the contest? Don't you want to win?" she asked, hardly able to believe what he was offering.

Tears streamed down his perfect cheeks. "Nothing is worth winning if it means losing you."

The breath caught in her throat. The man, terrified of being viewed as a failure, was ready to accept a life-changing loss all for her.

She blinked, coming back from the shock of his offer. "You'd do that? You'd give it all up? Your blog? The money?"

He smiled and cupped her face in his hands. "Do you need to hear this in the form of a royal decree from the esteemed Emperor of Asshattery?"

Now she was crying. "Yeah, I think I do."

He brushed a tear from her cheek. "With you by my side, Georgiana Jensen, messy bun girl, I'm not giving up anything. Don't you see, if you leave here with me, I've won."

Her trifecta broke out into fist bumps.

Tell him you love him!

She did love him. Somewhere between the Birkenstock teasing and the goat breakthrough and her brief stint back in the world of pub pageantry, she'd fallen in love.

She parted her lips. "I—"

"Stop! There's nowhere to run!" a man belted out.

Georgie gasped as the Dannies barreled toward them, limbs flailing. She pitched forward and fell into Jordan's arms as the siblings tore past them with a cadre of police officers and men and women in FBI vests in hot pursuit.

She gripped Jordan's arms. "What's going on with them?"

He shook his head. "I have no idea."

"We can shed a little light on that," Hector said, emerging from the murmuring crowd with Bobby by his side.

"Are the Dannies in some kind of trouble?" she asked.

"Yeah, it's not every day that you see the police and the FBI chasing people through a charity 10K," Jordan added.

"We've been keeping an eye on the Dannies and the Danny-Lyfe blog for some time," Hector began.

Bobby nodded excitedly and pushed up his glasses. "Their numbers were jumping at an insane rate."

"And Bobby and I were quietly looking into this when the

FBI contacted us. They'd been watching the Dannies, too," Hector added.

Georgie shared a surprised look with Jordan.

"It turns out, the Dannies were using click farms and bots to boost their followers. And they were stealing posts from smaller blogs and photoshopping themselves into pictures," Bobby continued.

Georgie turned to Jordan. "Do you remember when we saw them at the park? They said they'd been working with handicapped children."

"And there was barely a kid in sight," Jordan finished.

Georgie shook her head. "This is all crazy, but why would the FBI care about the Dannies?"

Hector shared a knowing look with his partner. "A couple of little things called fraud and tax evasion."

"The supplements," Jordan supplied.

"Bingo! They weren't reporting their income," Bobby answered.

Hector nodded. "And that's because they'd struck up a deal with Russian mobsters. They'd taken a bunch of their money to pay for all those click farms and bots that were supposed to boost the profile of the DannyLyfe brand. And that's not all. From what we know, it looks like they also spent some of it on lavish trips and lots of plastic surgery. They were selling the supplements, but they'd spent the money to do it right on themselves and ended up going with a sketchy supplement maker with a terrible track record. Those DannyLyfe energy supplements were nothing but baking powder and sawdust."

"That's awful!" Georgie exclaimed.

"But why did you invite them to participate in the Battle of the Blogs contest if you were already suspicious of them?" Jordan asked.

"This is where we got to go undercover," Hector said.

Bobby raised an eyebrow at his partner's words.

"Okay, not undercover, but we did get to help with the sting operation," Hector added, amending his statement.

"Here's how it went down," Bobby began. "We agreed to help the FBI and buy them some time to collect more evidence against the Dannies, while we did our own in-house investigation on the Dannies' online dealings. The plan was to lure the siblings into participating in the contest in hopes of winning the prize money. The FBI said the Dannies didn't have much liquid cash and needed to make a payment to the gangsters supporting their lifestyle. They knew their time was running out and hoped to win this contest and collect the prize money today to hand over to the mobsters tonight to try and get an extension on paying back all that they owed."

"Wow!" Georgie replied, stunned by the news, then gasped. "So, this contest was some elaborate scheme to catch a couple of crooks?"

"Kind of," Hector answered.

"Kind of?" Georgie and Jordan echoed back.

"We never wanted one winner," Bobby replied.

"What did you want?" Jordan asked.

Bobby fiddled with his glasses. "Isn't it obvious?"

She shared a *what the hell* look with Jordan.

"No," they answered in unison.

Bobby chuckled. "We wanted both of you."

A wide grin stretched across Hector's face. "Bobby and I love a good twist."

"And we always love a good opposites-attract story," Bobby continued, wrapping his arm around his partner.

"Initially, we were going to offer you both positions as paid contributors. But then we cooked up this idea with the FBI, and well, we couldn't wait to see what happened between the two of you," Hector explained.

"But I was the 'why date a ten when you should marry an eight' girl and Jordan was all about being a perfect ten."

Hector's grin stretched wider. "I know! Isn't it fabulous! It was like throwing yin and yang into a frying pan and waiting to see what happened."

"You've wanted it to be Georgie and me all along?" Jordan asked.

Bobby nodded. "Yes, and all those challenges just solidified how great you are together."

"Together?" she and Jordan replied.

"Like a 'He Said, She Said' thing. Call it whatever you'd like," Hector replied with a wave of his hand.

"Your numbers are through the roof. The whole CityBeat site is tittering on insanity, wanting to know if you guys are the real thing."

She turned to Jordan. "What about all your work building the Marks Perfect Ten Mindset blog?"

He smiled down at her. A smile so sweet, it nearly stopped her heart. "I kind of wrote a manifesto denouncing it."

"You did?"

"He also tried to withdraw from the contest," Bobby chimed in.

Jordan's gaze softened. "What do you say, Georgie? Could you be happy with a guy without a number?"

"I think I'm done with numbers," she answered, unable to look away.

Jordan caressed her cheek. "Good, because what we have is more than just a number."

"That's not bad," she said as Jordan frowned.

"What's not bad?"

She grinned up at him. "More than just a number. It's a great name for a blog."

He leaned in. "More Than Just a Number by Georgie Jensen."

"And Jordan Marks," she finished with Barry filming as their lips met in a kiss so sweet and so pure, no matter how many likes it got them, it was off the charts when it came to the metric of true love.

EPILOGUE

JORDAN

"Maybe if I bend my leg like that and put my knee over here, it will work. Can you check the book and see if I'm doing it right, Jordan?"

Jordan sat on the edge of the bed with Georgie between his thighs, which was, usually, exactly where he wanted her. Except, right now, she was upside down, doing a damn headstand with her knees hugging his head. And as much as he loved her knees and legs and every other part of her, he'd had about enough of trying the Kama Sutra's daredevil sixty-nine position.

He pushed the book aside and set her right-side up onto his lap. Rosy-cheeked, most likely from all the blood that had to have rushed to her head, her hair fell past her shoulders in loose waves.

She gave him a sexy little smile. "Not up for erotic acrobatics?"

"I was thinking more along the lines of this," he said, taking her hair into his hand and twisting her locks into a sexy as hell messy bun.

"Oh, it seems that Mr. Marks wants the naughty librarian,"

she purred, biting her fingertip, then running it seductively between her breasts.

"Mr. Marks definitely wants the naughty librarian," he answered, gripping her ass.

She pressed her finger to her lips. "Quiet! There's no talking in the library, sir."

He leaned in and took her earlobe between his teeth. "What are the rules on screaming?"

She sighed as he licked and sucked her soft skin. "Why do you ask?"

"Because all the people trying to read in silence are going to wonder who Jordan Marks is when I make you come so hard that you call out my name."

She arched into him, rubbing her slick center over his erect cock. "Your dirty talk is better than poetry."

He flipped her onto her back, then held her slim wrists above her head. "How's this for poetry? Roses are red. Violets are blue. Hold on, messy bun girl. I'm going to fuck you."

She ran her tongue across her top lip hungrily. "Somebody needs to notify the poetry society of your erotic literary genius."

He grinned down at her and positioned himself at her entrance. "I'll take you moaning my name over winning a poetry award any day."

He thrust inside her sweet heat, both of them gasping as he filled her completely.

"How do you want it, Georgiana Jensen, my favorite naughty librarian?" he bit out, grinding his pelvis against her sensitive bundle of nerves just the way she liked it.

Her blue-green eyes darkened. "Hard and dirty."

Holy hell! He loved this woman.

Their lives weren't always a Kama Sutra sex party. Three months ago, the Battle of the Blogs ended with him declaring his love for Georgie to the world. They'd won the contest that wasn't really a contest, and the Dannies had been arrested. The con artists had tried to hide from the authorities in a nearby park by pretending they were mimes because that's the kind of shit-for-brains stuff one does when taking supplements laced with sawdust. But he and Georgie didn't waste one second worrying about the pill-peddling Barbie-bot frauds.

And saying that things moved quickly after that day was an understatement.

Overnight, he and Georgie had become household names, and the More Than Just a Number blog had been born. This was their baby, and he was ready to give it one hundred and ten percent. Georgie, on the other hand, while completely committed to More Than Just a Number, had also decided to maintain her Own the Eights blog because, well, she hadn't been an impulsively in love freak and deleted ninety-nine percent of her blog content.

Yeah, he'd done that.

But he needed a clean slate. He needed to wash away the bullshit Deacon had planted in his head over the past decade and become his own man. A man who wasn't ruled by the trappings of perfection and the hollow promise that looks alone could lead to true fulfillment.

And speaking of fulfillment, with Georgie, he had it in spades or eights or vegan cookie dough. By whatever measure, she was his, and he was completely devoted to her.

Wisps of her hair broke free from her bun as he rocked his body against hers. He gazed into her eyes, hardly able to believe this smart, witty woman loved him. She was the everything he never knew he needed all wrapped up in one hot-for-the-book-shop-owner body.

He'd even given up his rental and moved in with her. It made sense. Yes, they'd only known each other for a couple of weeks when they'd decided to shack up, but that was all the time it took for him to know that her heart was the one he wanted to protect until his last breath.

And it made sense. They weren't only boyfriend and girlfriend. As co-creators of the More Than Just a Number blog, they were business partners, and thanks to the nice infusion of cash from CityBeat, they were neighbors on another front. They'd leased the ample office space next to Georgie's bookshop, and now, Marks CrossFit occupied a large portion of that space. And he didn't leave Deac's operation alone. Done with Deacon Perry's questionable business ethics, several of the best trainers from Deacon CrossFit migrated down the road to his new gym.

Life was good, really good.

He slid his hand to her hip and lifted her body, changing the angle of penetration as her hot center gripped his hard length. He drove into her in rhythmic, punctuated strokes, deep and hard. This was a take-no-prisoners sexpedition, and he growled into the crook of her neck, kissing her petal-soft skin.

"Jordan, don't stop!" she cried, her sultry gasps feeding his ravenous desire to make her body hum with pleasure.

"A ten always finishes what he starts," he teased, working her relentlessly as the slap of their sweat-slick bodies joined the chorus of her sweet cries and his low heated groans.

He released her wrists, and she clawed at his back then palmed his ass. Her hips meeting his, thrust for each fevered thrust, she was so close, and he knew just what she needed. Pumping his cock, hard and fast, he weaved his hand into her hair, gripped her now even messier messy bun, and tugged. The delicious combination of pulsing pleasure and the exquisite bite of pain was all it took to drive Georgie over the edge.

"Jordan Marks!" she called out as carnal victory surged through his veins.

Yep, if they ever decided to do this in a library, not even the patrons listening to audiobooks could ignore Georgie's primal cries.

Her nails carved tiny crescents into his ass as she writhed beneath him, meeting her climax in an intense rush of heat, and he couldn't hold back another second longer. He twisted the strands of her silky hair as their bodies collided in a torrent of raging passion. He met his release, grinding into her and lengthening her pleasure, while he disappeared into a world where only he and Georgiana Jensen existed.

Limbs tangled together, their bodies quieted, and he brushed his lips against hers, dropping whisper-soft kisses.

She opened her eyes and gave him a dreamy, sated smile. "You certainly do finish what you start."

He ran his index finger along her collarbone. "It's not very hard with the sexiest bookshop owner on the planet screaming your name."

Her rosy cheeks bloomed crimson. "I didn't scream."

He raised an eyebrow.

"I remarked with gusto," she clarified.

He bit back a grin. "Is that what we're going to call it? Remarking with gusto?"

A naughty glint sparked in her eyes, and a shot of lust surged through him at the thought of making her *remark with gusto* again, when their phones chimed at the same time, and Georgie gasped.

The official CityBeat contest had ended, but each member of this power couple, who not only collaborated on a blog but also owned their own businesses, had to be prepared for real-life challenges at the drop of a hat.

"Get Up and Move Storytime!" they said in unison.

"It's the first one, and we can't be late!" Georgie added, wiggling out from beneath him and springing from the bed.

He rolled over and propped himself up on an elbow. "We won't! That's why we set the alarms."

Since the bookshop and gym were right next door to each other, they'd decided to join forces and offer dual programs that incorporated literacy, Georgie's storytime, with physical fitness, child-friendly motor activities, held next door at his gym.

Georgie checked her reflection in the mirror and twisted her hair into another messy bun. "I cannot lead a storytime with sex hair, Jordan!"

He bit back a grin. He was sex hair's biggest fan.

"You look great. You always look great," he said, coming up behind her and dropping a kiss to her shoulder.

She met his gaze in the mirror. "You know I love you."

Yeah, he knew.

Pulling on clothes, they charged through their morning routine. Georgie opened the refrigerator and reached for a tube of vegan cookie dough, then shook her head and grabbed one of the kale smoothies he'd made last night.

"Am I ever going to like these?" she asked, taking a sip before calling Mr. Tuesday over and fastening his leash to his collar.

"It's an acquired taste, kind of like me," he replied, grabbing his smoothie, then opening the front door.

Georgie pushed up onto her tiptoes and planted a kiss on his cheek. "I'll take every flavor of Jordan Marks," she replied before Mr. Tuesday tugged on the leash and got them going.

It was a short jaunt through the neighborhood, taking less than ten minutes to hit the Tennyson Street business district. And look at him! Living the hipster dream, cohabiting with the woman he loved, walking to work, and drinking a kale smoothie while accompanied by a rescue mutt.

Oh, if Save the Whales Steve could see them now!

They rounded the corner and entered the bookshop, finding it packed with parents and children. Georgie had expanded the shop to include a kids and teen area, and today was its grand opening.

Becca waved them over to the counter. "Did you expect this many people?"

Georgie shook her head. "No, I just added the event to the bookshop's webpage yesterday."

"I guess you guys have to get used to all the notoriety. You two are famous now," Becca added with a sly grin.

She wasn't wrong. While they weren't A-list celebrity famous, people did recognize them all over town.

Georgie grabbed the picture book she'd chosen to read for today's storytime when a little boy holding a Dr. Seuss book walked up and tugged on the hem of her dress.

"Are you Georgie Jensen?"

She smiled down at the freckle-faced boy. "I am."

"Is this your bookstore?"

"It is."

"Is that your boyfriend?" the child continued, eyeing him.

Jeez! Georgie was a catch, and he figured there'd be some idiot who hadn't seen his post on CityBeat and would try to make a play for her, but he never considered he'd have to contend with dudes under four feet.

Georgie glanced his way. "Yes, he is. His name is Jordan. What's your name?"

"I'm Joey, and I'm in kindergarten," the little guy replied.

Georgie shook his little hand. "It's nice to meet you, Joey in kindergarten."

The little boy smiled up at her. "Would you like to marry me?"

Georgie's eyes grew wide. "I think I'm a little old for you, Joey. But one day, I'm sure you're going to get married and make someone very happy."

A flustered woman with an arm full of books joined them

and took the little boy's hand. "I'm so sorry. I hope my son wasn't bothering you."

"This is Georgie, and she's too old to marry me," Joey blurted.

Joey's mother blushed. "Oh, my goodness! Joey was the ring bearer in my brother's wedding this summer. Now, everywhere we go, he proposes marriage to the first pretty girl he sees."

The boy frowned and looked up at him. "Are you going to marry Miss Georgie?"

He froze. Like made of stone, caveman buried under eight layers of ice frozen.

Marriage? With all the craziness, the thought hadn't even entered his mind. It wasn't like he didn't love Georgie, and he wanted to spend eternity with her, but marriage was...huge.

"Yeah, are you going to marry, Miss Georgie?" Becca asked with her wry grin back in place.

"Come on, Joey," the woman said, guiding her son toward a display of children's picture books.

He and Georgie stared at each other, and from her shocked expression, it didn't look like she'd thought about it either.

Becca leaned against the counter. "Own the Eights gets married—just imagine that."

ALSO BY KRISTA SANDOR

Own the Eights Series

A delightfully sexy opposites attract/enemies to lovers series set in Denver, Colorado.

Book One: Own the Eights

Book Two: Coming Soon

Book Three: Coming Soon

The Bergen Brothers Series

A sassy and sexy series about three brothers who are heirs to a billion-dollar mountain sports empire.

Book One: Man Fast

Book Two: Man Feast

Book Three: Man Find

Bergen Brothers: The Complete Series+Bonus Short Story

The Langley Park Series

A steamy, suspenseful second-chance at love series set in the quaint town of Langley Park.

Book One: The Road Home

Book Two: The Sound of Home

Book Three: The Beginning of Home

Book Four: The Measure of Home

Book Five: The Story of Home

Sign up for my newsletter to stay in the loop and get in on all the big giveaways and contests! It's great fun!

https://kristasandor.com/newsletter-sign-up/

ACKNOWLEDGMENTS

When I decided to write a book about a bookshop owner and a CrossFit trainer, I knew that I'd need help. Luckily, one of my dear childhood friends is a CrossFit maven. Thank you, Sara, for pointing me in the right direction. It was tough work following all those ripped CrossFit guys you suggested I check out. But, I persevered—for the book. All kidding aside, thank you!

Dear readers, reviewers, bloggers, bookstagrammers, and ARC readers, thank you for giving me and my books a shot. So many of you have become close friends. I give thanks every day for our loving and supportive romance community.

Tera, Michelle, and Marla, you are the superheroes of editing and proofing. Thank you for making Own the Eights sparkle! I'd be lost without you lovely ladies.

Marisa-rose Wesley, as always, your work is awe-inspiring. Thank you for knocking the Own the Eights cover out of the park. I can't stop staring at it!

Brandi and Courtney, every time I message you and say, "Hey, want to read something?" You both always answer with an immediate yes! Thank you for your alpha-reader skills, feedback, and friendship.

Michelle Dare, my dear friend and mentor, thank you for your guidance. I thank the stars for you every day.

S.E. Rose, my BFF and writing partner in crime. I don't know what I'd do without you. You are a beacon of love and kindness. I can't wait for our next adventure.

David, my husband and my best friend, thank you for supporting me every step of the way. I love you.

To Denver, my adopted hometown and the city that owns my heart. Nineteen years ago, I packed up my little Geo Tracker and drove all the way from Miami to the Mile High City, and I've never looked back.

ABOUT THE AUTHOR

KRISTA SANDOR

If there's one thing Krista Sandor knows for sure, it's that romance saved her. After she was diagnosed with Multiple Sclerosis in 2015, her world turned upside down. During those difficult first days, her dear friend sent her a romance novel. That kind gesture provided the escape she needed and ignited her love of the genre. Inspired by the strong heroines and happily ever afters, Krista decided to write her own romance novels. Today, she is an MS Warrior and living life to the fullest. When she's not writing, you can find her running 5Ks with her handsome husband and chasing after her growing boys in Denver, Colorado.

Never miss a release, contest, or author event! Visit Krista's website and sign up to receive her exclusive newsletter.

Made in the USA
San Bernardino, CA
25 February 2020

64883287R00141